Alison Fraser

RUNNING WILD

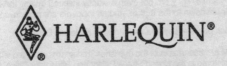

HARLEQUIN®

TORONTO • NEW YORK • LONDON
AMSTERDAM • PARIS • SYDNEY • HAMBURG
STOCKHOLM • ATHENS • TOKYO • MILAN • MADRID
PRAGUE • WARSAW • BUDAPEST • AUCKLAND

ISBN 0-373-18766-1

RUNNING WILD

First North American Publication 2001.

Copyright © 1996 by Alison Fraser.

Printed in U.S.A.

CHAPTER ONE

'WAIT till you see him. He's drop-dead gorgeous!'

That was the very first thing that Kip ever heard about Whit Delaney.

It wasn't said to her, but was part of the conversation going on between the two girls in front of her.

Kip didn't really know them, just their names. It was Lauren who'd spoken and Stacey who'd giggled in response. Both were blonde and attractive, each with a mouthful of perfect teeth.

'You have to be kidding!' Stacey declared. 'Prof Delaney's son could never be gorgeous.'

'Trust me, he is,' Lauren insisted. 'Ask anyone.'

Stacey glanced round, intending to do just that. Unfortunately the classroom was still half-empty, and her eyes fell on Kip as the nearest person.

Kip looked down but not quickly enough.

'Let's ask the English girl.' Stacey exchanged a sly smile with her friend.

Kip knew what was coming. She didn't know why but some girls had a compulsion to give her a hard time.

'Have you see him—the new lit. guy?' Lauren directed at her.

Kip shook her head. 'What's happened to Professor Delaney?'

Lauren rolled her eyes—a gesture copied by her friend. 'What planet do you live on?'

Kip didn't bother answering. It still puzzled her why if she left people alone they didn't do likewise.

'I know,' Stacey cried, 'Planet Reebok!'

Both girls laughed, inordinately amused by the joke.

It was lost on Kip, who never watched television, but she realised that it was a reference to her running.

'Professor Delaney had a heart attack at the half-semester,' Lauren informed her with a superior air.

'Oh.' Kip's green eyes clouded over. She'd liked the old professor. 'Is he all right?'

Lauren shrugged, his health of little importance compared with his son's appearance.

'Here he is!' she hissed at Stacey, and both girls instantly forgot about Kip.

Kip didn't care. She had made few friends at the New England college. With her training schedule and work commitments she had no time to socialise.

Mildly curious, she looked up with the rest. She hadn't expected to be impressed but Stacey was right. Professor Delaney's son was the handsomest man Kip had ever seen.

Well over six feet, he towered above the young male students in the room. His hair, a dark blond, was smoothed back from a high forehead and his face looked as if it had been cut from granite, then weathered by sun and storm. He could have been any age from thirty to fifty. It was irrelevant.

But it was his eyes that drew Kip's attention. An electric blue, they seemed somehow familiar—as if she'd met someone with eyes like that before.

Maybe it was just the effect they had; he glanced round the room once, took stock of the tutorial group, and, without saying a word, reduced them to silence.

'My name's Whitman Delaney,' he announced in dry New England tones. 'My friends call me Whit. You may call me Professor Delaney—unless you turn out to be a new, living Shakespeare, in which case you may call me Fool.'

There was a pause before the class dared to laugh. Kip didn't. She didn't like over-clever people. She was already missing his father—a gentle, absent-minded man who didn't demand too much.

'OK, essays.' He picked up a folder of papers. 'I call your name, you come and retrieve your masterpiece.'

So saying, he rapidly called names and at the same time comments. It seemed that Professor Delaney the younger took essay-marking more seriously than his father.

Fortunately for Kip there were fifteen other students in the group and he didn't notice the absence of a paper belonging to her. In fact she had high hopes of not being noticed at all. That was how she got through most lectures and tutorials in Radford College, a modest educational establishment in the state of Massachusetts.

Once or twice Kip thought that her hopes were about to be dashed, when his eyes alighted on her and rested there for a few moments, but each time they moved on, and eventually she relaxed and did what she normally did in tutorials: daydream.

The class was almost at the end of a discussion on great fictional acts of treachery when her luck ran out and he called out her name from a list. If he'd stuck to alphabetical order, Kip Wilson might have been safe to fight another day. As it was, she'd long since checked out mentally.

'Kipling Wilson?' He repeated the name when it elicited no response. 'Perhaps he'd like to identify himself?'

The mistake occasioned another round of laughter, as well as a smirk from Lauren and Stacey, the indistinguishable blondes in front of her.

Kip's dislike of Whit Delaney moved from vague to positive as she raised a half-hearted hand to acknowledge her name.

It was barely high enough to be observed. It was the eyes of the rest of the group that picked her out.

He arched his brows in mild surprise. 'Apologies. A she not a he.'

'How can he tell?' came in an overloud whisper from Lauren, and drew a malicious snigger from Stacey.

Kip remained untouched, though she understood well enough. While the American girls wore their hair long, waved and purposely tousled, Kip's straight black locks were as short as a boy's. But her face was clearly feminine, with wide, slanting eyes and a full mouth.

A boy had once dared to tell Kip that she was beautiful. She had laughed—a brittle sound of scorn. He had not told her again.

Now Whit Delaney gave her a smile of recognition. 'Ah, the runner. So traction wasn't required.'

It took Kip a moment to catch up with him, to register why his blue eyes had been familiar, then her thoughts travelled back a few days earlier to when she'd first met this man.

At seven in the morning the track had been shrouded in New England mist. That hadn't stopped her. She'd had a certain number of laps to complete before her classes. She'd been on the second to last when she collided into a solid object standing in her way. She'd gone flying.

'What the he—?' the solid object was also taken by surprise, but kept his balance.

Kip cursed too as she hit the ground then lay where she was. She didn't want to move until she was sure that she hadn't pulled, torn or broken anything.

'Are you OK?' Someone squatted down beside her. Intense blue eyes ran over her before a lazy smile appeared on an unshaven face.

Kip didn't see anything to smile at and continued to glower. He must have taken her expression as accusation for he stated the obvious. '*You* ran into *me*.'

'You *were* standing in the middle of the track!' Kip snapped in retaliation.

'True,' he conceded, watching as she rolled over and sat up. 'I guess I didn't expect any other joggers at this time of the morning.'

'I'm a runner, not a jogger,' Kip informed him witheringly. Not that he was withered in any way.

'I stand corrected,' he said, but on a mocking note.

Kip's temper didn't improve. 'This track belongs to Radford College,' she stated heavily.

'Yeah, I know,' he drawled in reply. 'So do I.'

Kip's eyes narrowed in disbelief. Radford had a number

of mature students but she'd never seen this man before, and he was definitely the noticeable type.

'I'm new,' he added at her suspicious look.

I bet, Kip thought sceptically, and asked, 'What's your major?'

He smiled. 'English literature—sixteenth to nineteenth century... What's yours?'

Kip didn't answer. She decided that the conversation had already lasted longer than necessary. She ignored his outstretched hand and lithely got to her feet. Then she gently stretched her leg muscles, warming them up once more, before she tried to finish her schedule.

'Perhaps we should go round together,' he suggested, 'to avoid any more collisions.'

'I like to run on my own,' Kip stated flatly.

He was unfazed by rejection, replying drily, 'That must make it difficult when you run competitively—or are you so far ahead that you don't notice the rest of the field?'

Kip knew that he was taking the mickey out of her by a suggestion of a smile in his deep blue eyes, but she didn't feel up to replying in kind. Instead she asked, 'How do you know I run competitively?'

'Just a guess.' He shrugged lazily, but his eyes were sharp enough. They took in her running gear of shorts and white sleeveless top, still emblazoned with the words 'Durham Harriers'—her old running club in England. They also took in the sweat plastering her hair to her face and making her top virtually see-through.

For a moment Kip felt aware of herself as a woman, but the moment passed, along with his interest. Kip should have been relieved but she felt the insult. With her body honed and toned for running she would not be regarded as sexually attractive—at least, not by this man.

When he said, 'You should be careful, running on your own,' it was in the nature of a warning, not a threat, as he too decided that he'd had enough conversation and left her.

Kip could hear his footsteps pounding on the track ahead of her and felt inordinately cross. She didn't like being patronised. She didn't like mockery, however gentle. And she didn't like tall American males who made her feel small.

She liked them even less, Kip decided now, when they turned into literature professors.

'OK, Kipling—' he repeated her name with a curious relish '—would you care to venture an opinion?'

'I...um...on what exactly?' Kip stalled for time, having only the vaguest idea of what had gone before.

'Whether Act Three turns the play from a comedy into a tragedy,' he responded helpfully.

Kip hadn't a clue. 'It's hard to say really.' She hedged once more rather than admit the fact that she hadn't read one word of the play they were discussing.

His gaze rested on her face for a long moment. Her cheeks went a revealing pink but her eyes were rebellious. It was a conflicting message.

No more conflicting, however, than his behaviour as he worked out the truth for himself...

'Very hard, I should imagine,' he commented drily, but then backed off and directed the question at someone else.

If Kip hadn't developed such a dislike for Whit Delaney, she could have kissed his hand in gratitude. As it was, she tried to escape out of the class the second it ended.

'Kipling!' He called her back before she could make the door. His voice was imperious. There was no chance of ignoring it. She reluctantly turned back. Stacey and Lauren tittered as they passed her.

Kip came to stand at his desk. He kept her waiting, putting papers away in an old, battered briefcase. Her expression was mutinous by the time his eyes switched to her.

She expected him to give her a hard time about being inattentive. Instead he went back to studying her.

'Who decided on Kipling?' he asked at length.

'What?' Kip blinked in surprise before answering. 'My father... Why?' she added cagily, forgetting his position as her teacher, remembering only the man she'd collided into on the track.

'No reason. It's not often I meet a fellow sufferer, that's all.' A wry smile touched his lips.

'Sorry?' His meaning escaped Kip.

'My father called me Whitman,' he explained, 'after Walt.'

'Walt?' Kip echoed before she could stop herself. Without intending to she was giving a fair impression of stupidity.

'Walt Whitman,' he stated patiently. 'American poet. The greatest ever, in my father's estimation.'

'Oh,' Kip replied lamely.

'But not in yours, I assume,' he said at her lukewarm reaction.

Kip could have pretended, but she had a feeling that this man would find her out soon enough. 'I've never read any of his work,' she admitted bluntly.

'Really?' He raised a surprised rather than mocking brow. 'Well, we'll have to rectify that. Meanwhile…Shakespeare, William? Great English playwright? You have heard of him?' he enquired drily.

'Just about.' Kip wasn't going to let him intimidate her.

'So?' He looked hopeful. 'What about that critique on one of his tragedies you wrote for my father?'

It was phrased as a question; Kip remained silent rather than lie.

She didn't have to. He knew already. 'At least, you were *meant* to write,' he ran on. 'Oddly enough, I don't recall reading it.'

From past experience Kip knew that it was better to confess earlier rather than later. 'I didn't quite get round to it… I told your fa—Professor Delaney.'

'Told him what, exactly?' Whit Delaney pursued.

'That I had a meet,' Kip mumbled.

'A meet?' he repeated, then answered for himself. 'A track meeting.'

'Yes.' She nodded. 'I had to train for it.'

'You're on an athletics scholarship,' he concluded. 'Well, that explains a lot.'

Kip wasn't slow; she realised what he meant. He thought

her a 'stupid jock', as college athletes were sometimes termed.

'OK, just so there will be no misunderstanding between us, Kipling—' his voice hardened '—some people reckon that if a kid can run a hundred metres in under ten seconds they should get a free ride through college. Unfortunately for you, I don't count in their number. You follow?'

'Yes,' Kip said through gritted teeth.

'So you owe me an assignment, right?' Sharp blue eyes held hers, waiting for an answer.

'Right,' she echoed, her face shuttered as he continued to study her. 'Can I go now?'

'When's our next tutorial together?' he enquired.

'Thursday.' Kip was already dreading it.

'Three days,' he calculated. 'Well, that should be sufficient time.'

'You want the essay by then?' she concluded in disbelief.

'Why, is that a problem?' He arched a brow, almost as if he was inviting her to argue.

Kip would have loved to, but she was fast realising that this man was going to be one major problem. She shook her head and this time didn't wait for a dismissal.

She stopped at the door, however, and asked, 'How's your father?'

Her concern was genuine but it obviously surprised him. Perhaps that was why he answered so directly. 'Still hospitalised but out of danger. They say he'll make a complete recovery if he does as he's told.'

'I'm glad,' Kip said simply.

'Shall I pass on your regards?' he suggested.

Kip nodded, then shrugged. 'He probably won't remember me.' And, muttering a final 'Bye,' she turned tail and ran.

Watching her go, Whit Delaney thought it unlikely that his father hadn't noticed her. Any good teacher would notice a kid who spent the whole lesson staring out of the window, wishing herself somewhere else.

Whit sighed himself, knowing the same feeling. He'd

agreed to keep his father's seat warm for him, but one day back in the job and he'd remembered why he'd quit in the first place. He enjoyed great literature; he didn't enjoy forcing it on kids who'd rather be reading the funnies—or, in that girl's case, running endless circles round a racetrack.

'How did it go, son?' his father asked when he visited him in the Radford Memorial that evening.

'Fine, Pops.' Whit didn't want to make his father anxious. It might have been argued that, at sixty, Alex Delaney should take heed of the warning his body had given him and retire, but the college was his life. If Whit didn't deputise for him, chances were that he wouldn't have a job to which to return.

'Liar!' his father said, no fool, and stated for him, 'You hated every minute.'

'Yeah, maybe,' Whit conceded, 'but don't worry. I can take it for a semester or two.'

'Thanks, son,' his father replied with quiet sincerity.

Whit shook his head, denying any need for gratitude. 'Just get better quickly, huh?'

'I will.' His father smiled, then went on to ask, 'So how's my little girl?'

'A living nightmare,' Whit answered, only half kidding. The little girl in question was his daughter, Abby, the apple of her grandfather's eye but the scourge of a dozen house-keepers. 'How long has Mrs Novak worked for you, Pops?'

'About fifteen years. Why?'

'Just wondering how far her loyalty might stretch.'

His father shook his head wryly. 'Mrs Novak won't quit. She's from strong New England stock. A few pranks from an eight-year-old aren't going to faze her.'

'We'll see.' Whit loved his daughter, but was more real-istic about her faults.

'She needs a mother,' his father declared. It was a familiar refrain.

'I didn't have one.' Whit remembered his own childhood as happy.

'And look how you turned out.' His father shook his head in apparent despair.

Whit smiled in response. Ten years of writing successful novels and his father had yet to congratulate him, but he knew that in his own way Alex was proud of him. In the same way, he loved and admired his father, resenting the students and lecturers who dismissed him as an old fogey.

The last thought triggered off a memory of his day and he said, 'There's a kid in one of your classes. Looks like a boy. Well, sort of, but not really. Quite pretty, in a way. Speaks with a put-on English accent.'

'Kipling.' His father smiled.

'Yeah, that's her,' Whit confirmed.

'It's not put on,' the older man declared. 'She's over from England on a scholarship.'

'I gathered the scholarship part.' Whit grimaced. 'An athletics one... I thought those bad old days were over.'

His father frowned, not understanding.

'Kids getting a free ride through college because they can throw a ball further or run a shade faster,' Whit added in disapproval.

'By and large, they are,' Alex Delaney claimed, but without denying that such practices existed.

'Well, no one appears to have got round to telling that English kid,' Whit continued disparagingly. 'She spent the whole tutorial gazing out the window, then looked aggrieved when I asked for the assignment she failed to do.'

'I believe she has problems,' Professor Delaney murmured in Kip's defence.

'Like?' Whit pressed.

'I'm not exactly sure.' His father shook his head. 'She doesn't say much.'

'You're not kidding.' Whit grimaced as he remembered the limited exchange he'd had with the girl.

'I'm surprised you noticed her so soon,' Professor Delaney ran on. 'She normally keeps a very low profile.'

'Yeah, well,' Whit answered drily, 'if you haven't even

read the play you're meant to be discussing, that's p
the wisest course.'

He didn't tell his father that he'd already met the girl on
an early-morning jog. He'd recognised her the moment he'd
entered the class and had expected recognition in return. She
had stared back at him blankly. It hadn't done his ego much
good, but that was his problem, not hers. The last time a
woman had been so cool with him he'd made the mistake of
marrying her.

'Go easy with her, son,' his father asked of him now, re-
ferring to this other English girl. 'You can be a little...hard-
nosed without realising it.'

Whit raised a brow but didn't disagree. 'I doubt my being
hard-nosed will bother your little English friend. She's not
so much remote as disconnected.'

'I'd noticed that,' his father mused. 'I just wonder why?'

'Well, don't worry about it,' Whit dismissed. 'She won't
be your problem for at least three months—and won't be
mine either, provided she meets her assignments.'

'Yes...' His father looked ready to tell him something but
then seemed to change his mind.

It was three days before he discovered what his father had
been going to say. On Thursday Kipling Wilson presented
him with her missing assignment, then kept her eyes fixed
rigidly on the floor until she could escape once more from
his class. He let her, mindful of his father's request to go
easy, but when he came to mark her work all thought of
being gentle went out of the window.

It was the worst piece of work that he had ever seen from
a college student.

CHAPTER TWO

'MISS WILSON, could you please wait?' Professor Delaney said as she tried to make a hasty exit out of the class.

Kip stopped and reluctantly turned. She'd hoped that she'd made it. He was surrounded by other students asking about their new assignment. But no, he'd still noticed her dive for the door.

She trailed back towards his desk and saw her essay on top of some papers. She knew what was coming. She'd been through this scene a hundred times.

She had to wait until he'd dealt with the others. She stood apart but listened as he gave pointers to more eager scholars. They seemed to like him, but then they weren't about to get their heads bitten off.

As his was the final class of the afternoon, the other students were in no hurry. But Kip was. She looked at her watch several times. She was caught doing it by Whit Delaney when he finally turned to her.

'I'm not keeping you, am I?' he drawled in the sarcastic tone that he seemed to reserve for her.

Kip thought what a stupid thing it was to say. Of course he was keeping her.

But she grated out, 'No.'

'Good, because this may take some time,' he warned as he reached for her work. 'I read your essay last night—or should I say I tried to read it?'

Kip waited for the familiar words. Stupid. Ignorant. Lazy. Insolent. She'd been termed them all, right back to the year she'd started school.

She remembered it distinctly. Her eagerness to join the

ranks of the other five-year-olds in their smart navy uniforms. Waving goodbye to her latest childminder—her dad had been too busy to take her. Almost running into that first classroom, with no qualms, because hadn't the grown-ups told her that she was too clever for her own good?

The shine on her hadn't lasted long. No child liked being shouted out. No child liked to be told that she wasn't trying when she was trying her heart out.

'How long have you been doing that?' Whit Delaney's voice brought her back to the present.

'Doing what?' she asked.

'Tuning out,' he flipped back.

He was so blunt that she found herself being blunt back. 'Since I was about eight.'

'Well, it hasn't done you much good, has it?' He rested appraising blue eyes on her and Kip felt her face redden. 'How old are you now?'

'Twenty-one.'

He raised a surprised brow. 'Older than the usual freshman. You don't look it.'

Kip knew that it wasn't a compliment so she said nothing. He was right, anyway. Most of the girls in Radford College dressed and made up to look older. Kip didn't care much about her appearance.

'So, isn't it about time you faced up to this thing?' he continued relentlessly.

Her stupidity, Kip assumed he meant, and she stared at him with a defiant gleam in her eye. 'I tried my best.' She glanced towards the essay that he had tossed back on the desk. The usual network of red lines had been applied to the top sheet.

'Maybe—' his tone was sceptical '—but it would have been more helpful if you'd just been up front from the beginning.'

'Up front?' Kip repeated warily.

'About your dyslexia,' he stated with stunning directness.

Kip stared at him in wordless surprise. She had spent years being told that she was stupid or lazy before someone had come up with a possible explanation. This man had discovered it on the briefest of acquaintances.

'You *are* dyslexic, aren't you?' he added at her silence.

Kip nodded and continued to stare at him. He had an angular face, hard-boned and uncompromising, with a jaw on the long side and a suggestion of a five o'clock shadow that only added to his masculinity. Dressed in jeans and checked shirt, he looked more like a character from a western than a literature professor. For a moment Kip felt her heart kick up a beat and she found that she was no different from other silly, susceptible girls.

But her face remained impassive. When his eyes caught and held hers, she denied any emotion and looked straight back at him. It was a mistake. Blue, mesmeric, his eyes were the sharpest that Kip had ever looked into; they saw all.

She found herself confessing, 'Yes, I'm dyslexic.'

He sensed her shame and said, 'It's not the plague, you know.'

'Oh, *I* know,' Kip replied with some of her usual spirit.

'Just other people don't seem to realise, huh?' he read from her tone.

Kip nodded again, at the same time trying to sort out her feelings. She'd disliked this man from the beginning and part of her still did. But his attitude to her problem was like a breath of fresh air.

'I assume the college is aware of the fact,' he went on.

This time Kip shook her head.

He looked puzzled. 'So how did you get away with that? Don't tell me they gave you an athletics scolarship without any academic credits at all?'

'I did an IQ test,' Kip explained. 'Mostly figures and logic problems. My major is computer science.'

'Can you cope with that?' he asked, frowning.

'With the work actually done on computer,' she confirmed, 'and the lectures and tutor groups. But not the manuals and textbooks—they require too much reading.'

'Yet you had a stab at *Hamlet*.' He indicated her corrected paper.

Kip bit her lip, then decided to come clean. 'I didn't read it. I got a cassette recording of it from the town library.'

'Enterprising.' His lips quirked in a smile for a moment before he ran on, 'Unfortunately, that's not going to get you through this course. An independent examiner may not take the time to decipher what you've written... To be truthful, neither did I.'

He fanned out her essay. Only the top sheet had been marked.

'I felt a sea of red pen would be counter-productive,' he said, 'but I do want to check what you've written, so I've arranged for you to see the department stenographer, Julia Barton.'

Kip frowned. 'I don't understand.'

'You dictate;' he explained briefly, 'she types.'

'Oh.' Kip stared at him in surprise. No other teacher had ever suggested such a thing.

'She's expecting you,' he added, handing her her essay.

'Now?' Kip's face fell.

'Now.' He nodded, and when she made no move to go quizzed, 'Is there a problem?'

Kip checked her watch. 'I have to be somewhere else.'

His face tightened. 'More important than this?'

Kip bit the inside of her mouth. She realised that Whit Delaney had put himself out for her. It had been many years since a teacher had. It was another chance, but she was going to have to blow this one too.

'Yes.' Steady green eyes offered him an apology.

He ignored it and made a gesture of impatience. 'The track, I assume.'

She shook her head.

'A boy, then,' he concluded next.

Kip frowned for a moment, not understanding, before shaking her head again. 'I don't date.'

'*You don't date?*' he echoed her matter-of-factness. It clearly amused him.

She found herself on the defensive. 'Is that so peculiar?'

'No, not at all.' He put on a straight face. 'Between you and me, I haven't dated for a while either.'

He gave her a smile. Kip didn't smile back. She felt that he was laughing at her—the same way as the other girls did.

'I have to go,' she announced, and didn't wait for permission this time as she took to her heels.

'You OK, kid?' Sam of Sam's Pizzas asked when she arrived at his restaurant, flushed and breathless.

She gave a small apologetic smile and answered indirectly, 'Sorry I'm late. I'll make it up.'

Kip didn't go into explanations. She kept college and work quite separate and, in some ways, felt more at ease in this life.

'Don't bother, kid,' Marcia, the other waitress on the shift, called out in greeting. 'He already gets more than his money's worth from you.' And, ignoring Sam's sour look, she ran on, 'My daughter's had her baby. A boy. Germaine. Like it?'

'Yes,' Kip lied kindly. 'Are they all right?'

'Swell. I've got a picture.'

'I'd like to see it.'

Marcia rummaged in her waitress dress's pocket, but before she could draw anything out Sam interceded, saying, 'She means later. Right now, if Grandma can shift her old bones over to table five and get their order, it would be much appreciated.'

'What a comedian!' Marcia muttered, being only forty and liking to pass for five years less than that, but she did as she was told, saying, 'Catch you later, kid,' to Kip.

'She will,' Sam warned Kip, having already had his fill of baby talk and photographs.

Kip smiled at both of them and went through to the back to slip on her waitress's uniform. She hadn't waited on tables before coming to the States but she'd picked it up quickly and worked as hard as any of the more mature waitresses. The fact was appreciated, and the rest treated her with an offhand kind of affection, calling her 'kid' rather than Kip, and, far from minding her quietness, used her as a sounding-board for their frequent personal troubles.

Even Sam had unbent towards her, having been initially reluctant to take on someone inexperienced, and when Kip had had to move out of the temporary accommodation that the college had arranged for her, he'd offered her the empty apartment above the pizza restaurant for a reasonable rate.

The restaurant was on the far side of town from the college but Kip had still taken it. Their customers were more what Sam termed 'regular folk' than students, but Kip didn't mind that; she didn't want to wait on the Staceys and Laurens of this world. And if 'regular folk' included the occasional drunk she could cope well enough with that. After all, she'd been brought up by one.

'I've got to hand it to you, kid,' Sam said at the end of another busy evening. 'You sure are good with awkward customers. The last student I hired didn't know squat about handling drunks.'

'Thanks.' Kip smiled at Sam's praise—almost extravagant for him—and called, 'See you tomorrow,' as she went out into the night.

She turned the corner and quickly climbed the outside steps to her apartment. It was really just one large, badly furnished room with an adjoining toilet where everything leaked. Kip's heart had dropped when she'd first seen it but now she hardly noticed its shabbiness. She spent so little time in it anyway.

It was midnight by the time she got to bed, and normally she slept the moment her head hit the pillow. Tonight, however, she couldn't seem to settle.

It was Whit Delaney, of course. She couldn't put him out of her head. He had understood, perhaps better than anyone, the mixture of pride and shame that made her conceal her illiteracy. He had offered her practical help, apparently in the belief that she *could* be helped. She knew that she should have been grateful—so why wasn't she?

She thought of the other students, boys as well as girls,

who crowded round his desk for attention. She didn't want to be like them. Worse, she didn't want to be on his list of worthy causes. She wanted—nothing, she told herself, refusing to acknowledge any feeling other than resentment.

Kip didn't usually feel sorry for herself, and she minded anyone else doing so. She had long ago accepted her problems with reading and writing. Perhaps they'd been made worse by her frequent school moves, but they'd been a fact of life too.

After his own athletics career had been brought to a premature end through injury, her father had coached her mother. After her death he'd quit athletics altogether and gone into leisure management. But his heart hadn't been in it and he hadn't seemed able to settle anywhere very long.

Kip didn't know when he'd started drinking. She couldn't remember a time when he hadn't. He had always been an amiable drunk—the kind that made dreams and plans and promises that never got past ramblings.

Except for the big dream. One day Kip was going to win the medal that her parents had both missed out on. Not just any medal. The ultimate. An Olympic gold.

It was the dream that had sustained Kip throughout what could only be termed an erratic childhood. At first it had just been words, something her father talked about at bedtime when other kids would have story books. But by eleven Kip was already showing signs that the dream could prove to be a reality.

Only it had been too late for her father, even then. He'd still talked of the dream, and at odd times had got involved in her training, but it hadn't been enough to keep him out of the pubs and clubs.

It had been Kip who'd kept going, even after she'd left school unqualified at sixteen and got a dead-end job in a factory. She'd joined a running club, and through it won her first important race just after her nineteenth birthday. Her father had been proud, of course. He'd spent a week celebrating, in fact, and had ended up on a hospital ward. It hadn't been the first time, but it had been the last. It had been too late to listen to the warnings of liver failure this time. He had put up no great resistance to death but had slipped away, holding her hand.

His only legacy had been the dream, but it had been enough. It had made Kip strong and got her this far. She wasn't going to give it up now. She wasn't going to let anything or anyone get in her way.

Barely five hours after she'd fallen asleep Kip was up and dressed and pacing herself round a track in the autumn chill. She ran every morning, every lunchtime, every moment she wasn't working or sleeping. It was a tough schedule but she didn't mind. Running was a physical pleasure—her legs gliding, her heart lifting, her mind and body flying, all cares left far behind.

It was on the track that she met Whit Delaney again. He wasn't running this time but sitting on one of the raised benches at the edge of the field. There was no mist this morning but she'd completed a couple of laps before she was aware of him. It was a week and a half since they'd last met, because Kip had simply stopped attending his classes.

Having recognised him, Kip kept running. She'd already done twenty laps. She went on to do another ten before exhaustion forced her to stop. He appeared at her side within moments. He wasn't dressed for running but in cream cords and flying jacket.

'Sick?' he enquired as she rested crouched over, hands on knees.

'Breathless,' she gasped.

'Not now,' he clipped out. 'Last week.'

It would have been easy to lie, say Yes, I've been under the weather, but what would have been the point? It could easily have been disproved. She'd gone to her computer lectures.

'No,' she replied when her breathing evened out.

'You just cut classes?' he concluded, hands on hips.

She straightened up. 'Yes. I realised you were right.'

'About what?' he flipped back.

'I'm not going to get through the course,' she admitted, then, shrugging, made to walk away.

He caught her arm, forcing her to stay where she was. Her eyes flashed him a look of protest. He ignored it.

'So you decide to quit,' he stated, his voice hardening, 'just like that.'

Kip didn't know why he was making such a thing of it. 'I thought you'd be pleased.'

'Well, you thought wrong,' he informed her. 'Apart from the discourtesy of not telling me—'

'I told my adviser,' she cut in. 'I assumed he'd tell you.'

'In the eye you did,' he threw back. 'You didn't give a damn one way or the other.'

He was right. She didn't. She was surprised that he cared. Or was it ego? Was he worried that her switching subjects would be seen as a reflection on him?

She eyed him stonily, then tried to pull her arm away. A silent struggle ensued. She pulled; he held; she gave up.

He changed tack. 'So, what are you taking as an alternative?'

'I...I haven't decided yet,' Kip admitted reluctantly.

'Well, when you do, let me know,' he countered. 'I'd be really interested in hearing what you can manage to study without being able to read or write past grade four.'

Kip's eyes shaded to black. There was no need for him to rub it in. She was already ashamed enough of her low reading age. That was why she tried to hide it.

She went on the attack, saying, 'What's it to you? Why should you care?'

'God knows,' he came back just as quickly, exasperated rather than angry. 'One of us has to.'

Kip shook her head. Didn't he understand? It had taken her years to learn how to *stop* caring.

He saw her anger become confusion, and, catching her eyes with his, added softy, 'I want to help you, Kipling... Let me.'

Kipling. No one had ever called her that, not even her father. It was like poetry on this man's lips. She saw the hand held out to her and wanted to take it. She felt her will being lost in the depth of his eyes.

Then he smiled at her and she thought, He's smiling at my weakness, and she was strong once more.

'I don't need this.' She rejected him, his concern, his help, and any softness in herself.

'Really?' His mouth straightened to cynicism. ''Cause you're going to be a world-famous athlete. Right?'

Kip's dislike went from mild to severe. Not only had he guessed her dream, he felt that he somehow had the right to ridicule it.

'Well, maybe you are,' he conceded, reading the suppressed anger in her rigid features. 'I hear you've got the potential.'

'Hear? Who from?' she demanded, at last pulling free of his hold.

'From whom,' he corrected her before responding. 'Your coach.'

'Mr Scott?'

He nodded at her alarmed look. 'Don't worry. I made it a general enquiry. I didn't tell him you're in danger of getting kicked out.'

'Am I?' retorted Kip.

'Believe it!' His face was deadly serious.

'You're going to report me,' she concluded.

But he shook his head. 'No, I'm not going to report you,' he contradicted her with an edge of exasperation. 'I won't need to. Paraphrasing what a famous American once said— you can't fool all the people all the time.'

'Abraham Lincoln.' Kip proved that she wasn't totally ignorant; she also accepted what he was saying. 'If I can survive a year, it'll be enough.'

'For what?' He followed her as she walked towards the changing rooms.

'To improve my time for the three thousand metres,' she

explained frankly. 'Get in the world's best hundred and I'm sure to get commercial sponsorship.'

'Then it's goodbye, Radford.' He made her sound hard and calculating.

Perhaps she was, Kip admitted, but she found herself defending her plan. 'If I make it into the fastest ten, I'll earn an awful lot of money. Any debt I owe Radford I will be able to repay.'

'So the bottom line is dollars and cents?' he drawled in disparaging tones.

Kip rounded on him and said in utter seriousness, 'No, the bottom line is an Olympic gold.'

He didn't scoff. He heard the gritty determination in her voice. It drew a deeply worried frown from him.

'And then?' he asked simply.

And then I'll be able to live, Kip thought rather than said, and frowned to herself. It was the first time she'd considered the future in those terms and she wondered for a moment what she meant. Before she could analyse it further, his voice broke into her thoughts.

'You won't get a year,' he stated with certainty. 'Radford may not be Yale or Harvard, but it still prides itself on an above-average academic standard. You aren't going to meet it.'

'Why are you telling me this?' Kip's face was stiff with resentment.

Whit Delaney asked himself the same question. Right at this moment he could be at home eating breakfast with his daughter and his father—now out of hospital. Instead he had chosen to get out of bed at some ungodly hour to track down this English kid. And for what? Not gratitude, that was for sure. She was looking at him as if he were something that had crawled out from under a stone.

'Someone has to,' he growled back, 'unless you want a one-way trip back to…Manchester, isn't it?'

Kip started in surprise at this. Of course the college had a file on her, but it listed her last digs as Newcastle. Somehow he'd guessed that she'd spent a large part of her childhood in the Manchester area.

'I was a Rhodes scholar,' he explained.

Kip's blank look confessed her ignorance.

'I spent a couple of years studying at Oxford University,' he added, 'where I acquired a minor talent for identifying accents. Was I right?'

'Sort of.' She didn't want to go into her background. She wanted to end the conversation there, in fact. 'I have to go and change.'

The sweat had dried on her skin. He saw her shiver. Her body had dropped in temperature while they'd been talking.

Whit Delaney studied her for a moment. Her hair was short like a boy's and her figure athletic rather than slim, yet she was surprisingly pretty. Possibly more than pretty, if one took into account those large green eyes and the full mouth.

Was that why he was bothering? Because he found her attractive? Whit shook his head at the idea. No, even if she hadn't been one of his students, she was too young and too much trouble. This girl had the words 'hard time' written all over her.

Yet he still found himself saying, 'I'll see you in class later.'

He made it sound like a threat, though the truth was that he hadn't got round to planning what he'd do if she didn't show.

The full mouth tightened into a thin line. She looked as if she'd like to tell him to go take a hike. She just couldn't afford to.

She turned away without a word, but her back was rigid with pride. He wondered if she would materialise that afternoon. If she didn't, he decided, he wouldn't take it any further. The college authorities would find her out sooner or later, without his help.

He walked away from the stadium, through tree-lined streets to the wooden clap-board house on Washington Avenue where his father lived.

'Daddy!' his daughter, Abby, called excitedly when he appeared in the kitchen, then followed the greeting with an immediate demand of, 'Where have you been? Gramps isn't getting up till later, and you weren't in bed this morning!'

She looked accusingly at him.

'I went for a jog,' he claimed without thinking.

Abby saw through him straight away. 'In those clothes?'

She was one smart eight-year-old, Whit knew. He also knew that he was going to have to do something about her soon. She could so easily become a spoilt, petulant brat—like her mother.

He caught Mrs Novak's eye. His father's housekeeper for well over a decade, she allowed herself liberties. This time it was to mutter, 'Some people are no better than they ought to be.'

Unsure whether it was directed at him or Abby, Whit did the sensible thing and ignored it.

'Good morning, Alice.' He greeted the woman with a wide, handsome smile.

It elicited a 'huh' but a pink colour rose in Alice Novak's cheek before she announced, 'Breakfast was ready twenty minutes ago.'

'Well, it still looks delicious,' Whit said pacifically, sitting by the plate that was slapped down at his usual place. He didn't have to lie about that one. Mrs Novak was a good cook. Too good. That was why he'd taken up jogging again and met Kip Wilson in the first instance.

He found himself thinking about the girl again. He wondered why she interested him. Was it because she reminded him of Elizabeth? She didn't really. Only in that she was English. But there the comparison ended.

His thoughts switched to his ex-wife, Elizabeth Clayton. He'd heard about her before he'd met her. A young, up-and-coming English actress, perfect for the female lead. She'd been the director's choice but Whit's opinion had been sought. It had been his book—his first to be bought by Hollywood—and he'd done the screenplay adaptation. The heroine had been loosely based on a girl he'd met during his time at Oxford, but more rooted in a young man's fantasy of the perfect woman.

And Elizabeth Clayton had been its embodiment. Beautiful. No, beyond that. Exquisite. Hair like golden thread, skin like alabaster. A figure as graceful as those of the women in a Gainsborough painting. And a voice like silk. He'd had to have her—or what he'd thought she was, at least.

No, there was no comparison between Elizabeth and Kip Wilson. She was just some skinny kid with a large problem and an even larger chip on her shoulder. She interested him purely because he'd never met anyone quite so antagonistic.

'Dad, I've decided.' Abby broke into his thoughts once more. 'I don't really want a new mommy.'

'What?' Whit did a double take.

'You weren't listening!' Abby accused him, then stated plaintively, 'No one listens to me.'

'I'm not surprised,' Alice Novak muttered in one of her loud undertones.

'I was listening,' Whit claimed. 'I just wasn't sure I heard right. Who said anything about new mommies?'

'Katie Day,' Abby announced importantly.

Whit raised a brow. 'And who's she when she's at home, kiddo?'

'Only *the* most beautiful girl in my class,' Abby declared with a mixture of envy and admiration. 'She knows all about new mommies and daddies. She's had lots, and they all suck!'

Whit winced a little at Abby's turn of phrase but decided to let it go. She either didn't know what she was saying, in which case it didn't matter, or she did and was saying it for effect, in which case it would be better to underreact.

It was Alice who declared with menace, 'Soap and water!'

Whit understood, responding drily, 'Why don't we go the whole hog and tar and feather her?'

'What do you mean, Daddy?' Abby turned hostile blue eyes on the housekeeper, her sworn enemy.

'Nothing, mugwump,' Whit dismissed. 'Just a joke.'

Alice snorted, showing that she wasn't amused.

Abby snorted too—a mannerism picked up directly from the housekeeper—before departing with, 'I'm going up to say goodbye to Gramps.'

'Look, Alice,' he said, turning to the housekeeper, 'I know she's a handful right at present, but give the kid a break. She's not had it so easy.'

Alice bridled in the first instant, then sighed, 'I know. I'm sorry. It's just...well, the child doesn't like me and that makes it hard.'

'Yes.' Whit didn't deny it. Abby had disliked all the housekeepers that he'd hired too. 'But it's not personal to you, Alice, and it's not really Abby's fault either. She's just had too many changes in her young life.'

'I suppose so.' Alice didn't know all the details, but she'd gathered that Abby Delaney had been bounced between parents like a tennis ball. 'I want to be sympathetic, truly I do, but she does try my patience,' she admitted wearily.

'I understand that,' Whit consoled her, 'which is why I've been considering hiring a student for a couple of hours after school to keep her out of your hair. What do you think?'

'I...well, I'm not sure.' Alice was hesitant.

'She won't have anything to do with the running of the house,' Whit assured her. 'She could take Abby swimming or something.'

Alice Novak brightened. 10 Washington Avenue was her province. She wanted no other woman interfering. But some young slip of a girl? That was another matter.

'I think that might work out all right,' she conceded.

Whit smiled and went through to his father's study while the idea was fresh in his mind.

He had some notion of the sort of girl that would suit. Which made it all the more strange that he kept picturing Kipling Wilson. For she was the last person he would choose, surely?

CHAPTER THREE

THE class was buzzing with the news. Once again Kip learned it from Stacey and Lauren.

'You haven't applied, have you?' Lauren demanded of Stacey.

'Too right I have,' Stacey declared, looking pleased with herself.

'But why?' Lauren was still incredulous. 'You don't need the money. Your dad sends you anything you ask for... And you can't really want to babysit some snotty-nosed kid.'

'Not any snotty-nosed kid,' Stacey corrected her. 'Professor Delaney's snotty-nosed kid.'

'That's just speculation.' Lauren had read the advert on the notice-board too. There was no name, no address, just a telephone number.

Stacey shook her head. 'Not any more. I called.'

'You talked to him?' Lauren asked disbelievingly.

'No, to some housekeeper,' Stacey admitted. 'But it's his kid all right, and I reckon I'm in with a pretty good chance. Just you wait.'

'I believe you,' Lauren responded. 'I just can't see you hanging round with a kid for a couple of hours every afternoon.'

Stacey shrugged. 'It won't be that bad, and some things are worth the sacrifice.'

'You really think you stand a chance with him?' Lauren looked sceptical once more. 'Isn't he a bit old for you?'

'I like my men mature,' Stacey boasted with a superior smile, 'and I'm willing to bet the prof likes his women young. Everyone knows that's what attracts college types to the job in the first place: the opportunity to drool over young, nubile bodies.' Stacey languorously stretched her own.

'I don't know.' Lauren was still doubtful. 'Somehow I don't see Professor Delaney as the drooling type.'

But Stacey just gave a confident laugh. 'All men are, believe me!'

Kip tried not to listen to their conversation but it was difficult. It was both repellent and fascinating at the same time. Like Lauren, she couldn't imagine Whit Delaney drooling, yet Stacey's confidence was absolute. She found herself wondering if Stacey could possibly be right as Whit Delaney strode into the tutorial.

His eyes went straight to the back of the classroom and Stacey acknowledged his interest with a wide, perfect smile. Kip, for her part, dropped her gaze and stared at her desktop, hoping and praying that he would choose not to notice her reappearance.

She had come back to his classes because it seemed easier to do so. Sure, he knew her secret, but chances were that any other teacher would in time. And she had done the work he'd asked, so maybe he would now leave her alone.

He certainly didn't direct any questions at her on the current text, which was just as well. There was no library tape for the particular play they were studying and she'd struggled for hours to read a single act, let alone grasp any deeper meanings.

At the end of the lesson she didn't duck out of the classroom but approached his desk. As usual, keener students had gathered to hear more words of wisdom. It was little wonder that he was big-headed.

He noticed her over the tops of the others' heads and he offered her a seemingly genuine smile.

'Good to see you again, Miss Wilson,' he said with only a hint of irony.

Kip almost smiled back, but then changed her mind. She didn't want to join his fan club. Nor did she want to be considered the black sheep, allowed back into the fold. She just wanted to survive.

'I've done the assignment.' She handed him her essay.

He looked surprised. 'You had it typed.'

She nodded, then admitted, 'Not at college. Someone else did it.'

'A friend?' he suggested.

Kip shook her head. She'd seen the card in the delicatessen a few doors down from Sam's Pizza—'Typing at reasonable rates'. It had been an old lady with an equally old typewriter and it had taken hours for Kip to dictate the essay.

'Well, I appreciate the effort.' He slanted her a warm, approving smile.

It breached Kip's defences and she responded in kind. Kip's smiles were rare and sudden—and transformed her face to beauty.

Caught by surprise, Whit murmured aloud, 'Like sunshine after rain.'

Perhaps she didn't understand the comment. She looked confused, all eyes, which were vivid green in her thin, small-boned face.

He remembered who they were—teacher and pupil—and added, 'Sorry, that was out of line.'

Kip stared at him a heartbeat longer. No one had ever compared her to sunshine before.

She found herself blushing, then muttering, 'I have to go.'

She didn't wait for permission but took off, alarmed by the chaos of her emotions. How could she feel drawn to this man when he made her so angry most of the time?

She was going to be late for work, but she knowingly ran in the wrong direction, down corridors to the notice-board. It took her a moment to locate the card and a while longer to read it.

COMPETENT BUT CARING BABYSITTER
REQUIRED FOR EIGHT-YEAR-OLD GIRL
LATE AFTERNOONS AND SOME WEEKEND
WORK
EXPERIENCE PREFERRED
SALARY NEGOTIABLE

She wasn't sure why she had to read it. She wasn't going to apply. She didn't know how to care for a child—or anyone else for that matter. She'd been on her own too long. And she liked it that way.

Whit Delaney would never employ her, either—Kip realised that. An English professor wasn't going to employ someone with a reading age in single figures to mind his daughter.

Curiosity. That was what had driven her, but that in itself was unusual. She'd ceased being curious about people at the time when she'd discovered how much she disliked people being curious about her. But no one had ever shaken her up the way Whit Delaney did.

Other students appeared at the notice-board and she turned away, as if caught doing something wrong. She raced to Sam's Pizzas and, in running, blocked out thoughts of anything else.

She made it just on time, and, it being Friday, their busy night, she remained on her feet until midnight. If she thought of anything, it was of the race tomorrow. The athletics team was competing in a meet at a college some fifty miles distant. It wasn't a particularly prestigious event and it was unlikely that there would be any of the big professional coaches in attendance, but it was still important for her to get some races in.

That was what Bill Scott, her athletics coach, had told her, and she knew it to be true. She could race against a clock; since coming to America and having more time to train, she had knocked minutes off her personal best. The trouble was in competition. Put her on a field with other runners and she lost the rhythm in her stride and the determination in her heart. It was as if she didn't want to beat other people, just herself.

'You can do it,' Bill Scott told her seconds before the race on Saturday. 'There's no one faster on this track today. I believe in you. Believe in yourself.'

'Thanks, coach.'

Kip liked Bill Scott. He understood about running and how

important it was to her. It was for him too. That was why he gave her individual coaching in non-college hours. He shared her dream that one day she would run in the Olympics.

That day seemed a little closer this afternoon. With Bill Scott's words in her ear, Kip ran a brilliant race. She let the pacemaker do her job, resisting the temptation to overtake and run her own race. She stayed tucked behind the leading pack until the final bell, then the jostling began—a scramble for the first three places that often found her nowhere. But not today. She kicked up a pace, got clear and stayed out in front all the way to the tape.

Bill Scott was jubilant. Kip was drained. She'd wanted to win until the second she'd crossed the line, then there had just been that feeling of anticlimax, dragging her spirits down to rock-bottom.

Bill didn't notice. He was talking nineteen to the dozen: plans, the future—the sky was the limit. Winning excited him in a way that it never did with Kip.

'We're getting there,' he said as the team bus sped homewards, 'but you're going to need to work on your race psychology, and you can't do that running round an empty stadium at five o'clock in the morning.'

'I'm following your schedule,' Kip replied to the criticism in his voice.

'I know, kid, I know,' he assured her. 'Between ourselves, I've had my ear chewed about the fact.'

'Who by?' Kip frowned.

'Alex Delaney's son.' He pulled a face, then, remembering that she was a student not a colleague, added, 'Professor Delaney. He's your English tutor, I understand.'

'Yes. He doesn't like runners.' Her eyes blazed at his interference.

'Whit?' Bill Scott questioned in surprise. 'I don't think it's that. In fact, he was a bit of an athlete in his own time. Might have taken it more seriously if he'd been less talented in other ways. He's a Harvard grad, no less. Don't get many of them at Radford.'

Kip said nothing. Bill clearly liked Whit Delaney.

'Anyway, maybe the boy's right.' Bill forgot her student status once more. 'Maybe solitary training at unsocial hours is the quickest route to burn-out.'

The 'boy', Kip assumed, was Whit Delaney. It was not what she would have called him.

'He's certainly right in part,' Bill continued. 'You need to train with everyone else, if only to get used to sharing a track.'

'I can't.' Kip stated what Bill already knew.

It was partly down to Bill Scott that she was here. Until six months ago she had been a packer in a clothing factory, had lived in digs in Newcastle and run in the evenings with an amateur club. One of the older members, Colin Evans, had known her father. He had also known Bill; he was married to Bill's sister. Between them they had arranged for her to come to America and train.

But money was still a problem. The scholarship barely covered fees, books and the specialist running shoes she needed. She'd blown her entire savings on a one-way air ticket. The job at the pizza parlour was vital to her.

'Can't you ask your boss if you can start later?' Bill suggested.

'I asked before,' Kip shook her head, revealing the answer.

'Well, it's no good the way things are,' Bill declared. 'You're going to have to get another job.'

'I can't,' Kip countered. 'I'll lose the apartment.'

Bill sighed, acknowledging her predicament. 'I know it's tough, kid. I wish I could help you myself…but you've got to accept it. If you're serious about your running, you have to attend training sessions like everyone else. Apart from anything else, it would help you develop a little team spirit.'

Kip made no comment. It wasn't the first time Bill had implied that she was too much a loner. She couldn't defend herself. She *was* a loner, and had been as far back as she could remember. Each time her father had moved jobs and she had moved schools she had grown a little more reserved and a little less inclined to make new friends, until eventually she'd given up.

Bill saw her strained expression and felt that he'd been too hard on her. 'Never mind, kid; you did us proud today,' he said on a more upbeat note, and, giving her arm a quick squeeze, went off down the bus to dispense advice to his other athletes, winners and losers alike.

Kip returned to staring out of the window, not thinking of the race that day, or Bill's advice, or the week ahead. Instead her thoughts were on Whit Delaney as she nursed her anger at his interference.

The anger lingered even after a few days had passed. She still felt it when she went to his next tutorial, although she didn't look at him once.

He ignored her too, until the very end. Then, after he'd given them a new assignment, he added, 'Kipling, could you stay back for a moment?'

Kip's heart sank. She didn't feel up to one of his pep talks.

Lauren didn't improve her mood either as she said in an overloud voice, 'It's a pity you aren't the class dork, Stacey; then you'd get to wait behind too.'

'Rather pointless,' Stacey replied. 'He's hardly likely to be interested in a retard.'

They both glanced behind to make sure that their words had hit their target.

They both stared in amazement as Kip retaliated with an abrupt 'Get stuffed.'

It was one thing that Kip had learned in the inner-city schools she'd attended as a teenager: ignore trouble unless it went looking for you, then face it down or go under.

'What did you say?' Stacey eventually gasped.

'You heard,' Kip retorted. 'Just back off!'

Lauren did as she suggested, but not before muttering to Stacey. 'She can't speak to you like that.'

Stacey would have liked to back off too, but she couldn't without losing face. Their fellow students had already been drawn to the little scene.

'Or what?' she said—a challenge that came out as more of a squeak.

Kip showed no fear because she had no fear. 'Or book in for another nose job,' she suggested in dangerously low tones.

Colour flooded Stacey's face as she spluttered, 'Are you trying to say I've had cosmetic surgery?'

Kip remained cool, her eyes running over the other girl's face. 'Now I come to think about it, probably not.'

The insult was there and Stacey didn't have to look too hard for it. 'Why, you…'

She took a step towards Kip. Kip didn't flinch. She was ready, one hand clenched in a fist. She'd had to fight before—fight or get beaten.

It was then that Whit Delaney stepped in, cutting through the small crowd round them. He looked at the English girl's face. It was a pulse or two away from explosion. He looked at her opponent—the rather gushing girl he'd accepted as a babysitter.

'What's going on here?' he said to both, but his eyes went automatically to Kip.

The shutters came down. She said nothing. It was Stacey who lisped the words, 'I don't know, Professor. We were just discussing the assignment and the next moment she's calling me names.'

'Is this true?' he directed at Kip.

'No.' She met his stare with a level look of her own. 'I didn't call her names. I told her to get stuffed.'

A general murmur went round the crowd at this stark admission, then Stacey, smelling victory, added plaintively, 'And she implied I'd had a nose job.'

This was obviously the major crime in this girl's view. Whit had an inappropriate desire to laugh. He controlled it and glanced towards Kip.

She said nothing. Instead she looked bored, as if she had already disconnected herself from the scene.

Whit shared her feelings and might have left them to their quarrel but for the fact that it involved Kip. He hadn't imagined all that anger, hidden now by her air of cool. She was dangerous.

'Right. Take off,' he directed at Stacey and the other students still hanging around.

They did, slowly, reluctantly, cheated of a little excitement.

'Not you,' he added, as Kip made to leave too.

The look of simmering anger returned to Kip's eyes but she didn't protest. Instead she folded her arms and waited, ready to replay a familiar scene.

He folded his arms too, and they eyed each other for a moment or two before he enquired, 'Do you want to put your side?'

'No.' Kip assumed that she'd already been judged.

'Fair enough.' He nodded and, giving a shrug, walked back to his desk.

Disconcerted, Kip followed and waited for sentencing. When he said nothing more she eventually prompted, 'What do you mean to do?'

'About what?'

'Me facing down Stacey.'

He stopped shuffling papers and gave her a sardonic look. 'Is that what you call it? I'd say intimidating the hell out of her was nearer the mark... What would you like me to do?'

Kip scowled. Did he expect her to answer that?

Apparently not, because he ran on, 'Look, kid, if I wanted to play referee I'd get a job teaching tenth grade in downtown New York. If you and Stacey have a problem with each other, that's your business.'

'*I* have no problem,' Kip claimed heavily.

'Good.' He dismissed the subject abruptly and held out her essay instead. 'As was this. Very good.'

It lasted a second, her rush of pleasure, quickly killed off by the hard look on his face.

'The only question,' he went on coldly, 'is who wrote it?'

'What?' Kip stared at him in disbelief, then she protested indignantly. 'No one... I mean, *I* did.'

'And I'm the president of the United States,' he countered drily. 'Look, kid, you were in a hole and you found someone

else to dig you out. You aren't the first person to pay for a
little ghosting.'

It was a moment before Kip unscrambled what he was
saying. He thought that she had paid someone to write the
essay for her.

'*I wrote it!*' she repeated, her face flushing with anger.

He took it to be guilt and said with a sarcastic edge, 'If
you can have ideas this original, Miss Wilson, then it's a pity
we never hear them in class.'

Kip saw his point. She spent his classes doodling or day-
dreaming. Having been written off early as a dunce, she'd
reacted by switching off. This essay represented one of the
few times when she had really tried, which was why she was
angry—so angry that she was trembling with it.

'I wrote it!' she insisted hoarsely, her eyes furious.

Whit registered the strength of her reaction and wondered
whether she knew what was true any more.

'Listen, kid—' he adopted a more patient air '—I read the
top page of the essay you gave me a couple of weeks ago. I
may not remember it word for word, but this isn't it.'

'I wrote it again,' Kip replied heavily, 'because I had to.
I couldn't read my own essay to dictate it, so I got out the
play from the library again and used a recorder to tape a new
essay which Mrs Steenburg typed. I still have the recording
at home.'

'Who's Mrs Steenburg?' He still sounded sceptical.

'A typist,' she explained briefly, 'who lives round the corner from the pizza parlour.'

'The pizza parlour?' he echoed quizzically.

Kip offered no explanation but looked at her watch again.
Once again he'd made her late. 'I have to go.'

'Uh-uh!' He grabbed her arm when she would have done
one of her escapes on him. 'Not till we sort this out. You
can either confess now and I drop the matter or we can go
discuss it with the principal.'

Kip tried and failed to slip from his grip. Her scowl told
him what she thought of the choices, but she saw little point
in claiming her innocence any more.

'All right, I paid someone.' Kip said what he wanted to hear. 'Can I go now?'

He made no reply. He continued to study her face, as if searching for some understanding of her.

Kip didn't want to be understood by this man. She wanted to run and keep running. 'Look, I have to go home...I'm late,' she appealed through gritted teeth.

'Yeah, OK,' he said, but he didn't release her. Instead he hooked his suede jacket off the back of his chair. 'I'll give you a lift.'

'What?' Kip looked at him in shock.

'I'll give you a lift,' he repeated. 'Then you won't be late... Whereabouts do you live?'

'Across town,' she replied vaguely, adding, 'I don't need a lift. I'll run it.'

'I insist.' He kept hold of her arm and steered her towards the door. 'Have you anything to collect from your locker?'

Kip shook her head and would have shouldered her bag of books but he took it from her.

They walked down the corridor in silence, Kip conscious of the fingers curled tightly round her bare arm. Her heart beat hard against her ribs as she considered putting up a fight for her freedom.

They reached the staff car park before she could make her move, then it seemed simpler just to go along with him. Radford wasn't a big town by American standards. It wouldn't take long for him to drive her home.

He came to a halt in front of a sleek sports car and she was surprised into saying, 'It's a Jaguar.'

'Yes.' He didn't hide his pride in the car. 'A 1950s model. Imported from England, like yourself, and arguably more trouble than it's worth.'

As they got in Kip wondered if this last observation was intended to apply to her as well as his car. 'You don't have to give me a lift,' she stated coldly.

'No, I don't,' he agreed, at the same time putting the car into gear and reversing out of his parking space. 'Address?'

Kip gave it, and started to give directions, but he interrupted, 'It's OK; I know it.'

Kip was surprised. She lived in an area of town that was
exclusively working-class. Few students chose to live there,
and no staff.

'I was brought up in Radford,' he explained, 'and it hasn't
changed much in the decade or two since I've been away.'

'Where do you normally live?' Kip found herself asking.

'For many years it was New York, but recently I bought
a house on the Maine coast,' he related. 'I guess we'll return
there when my father gets better.'

'Which does your wife prefer?' Kip assumed that he was
married from the existence of a daughter.

'My wife's dead,' he stated without emotion. 'While she
was alive she preferred Paris or London or pretty much anywhere I wasn't... The "we" I mention is my daughter and
myself.'

'Oh.' Kip wished that she'd kept her mouth shut. 'What's
your daughter's name?' she asked, searching for safer
ground.

'Abigail,' he revealed. 'Abby for short. A singularly inappropriate name for the tough little cookie she is... You
should meet her. You'd probably get on,' he added, smiling.

Kip doubted it. 'I don't really like children,' she stated
bluntly.

It drew a surprised look, then a brief laugh. 'Well, that's
honest at least. For the last week I've been interviewing a
score of young women, all claiming to be a reincarnation of
Mary Poppins. I'm looking for a babysitter for my daughter,'
he explained.

'Yes, I saw your advert,' she admitted.

'And decided to give it a miss,' he concluded drily.

'I have a job,' she countered.

He glanced across at her. 'Doing what?'

'Waiting on tables.' She dared him to look down on her.

'Pity,' was his only comment. 'You might have been just
what Abby needs—someone as tough as herself.'

Kip's lips compressed, betraying annoyance. She didn't

deny being tough. She had survived because of it. But for some reason she didn't want this man giving her points for it.

'Where exactly?' They had finally reached her street.

'Drop me anywhere,' Kip suggested.

'Where exactly?' he repeated, and at her obvious reluctance assured her, 'Don't worry, I won't invite myself in for coffee.'

'At the pizza parlour.' She pointed up ahead. 'I live above it.'

He turned off the main street and parked by the steps to her apartment. He looked up at the narrow alley of bins and blowing rubbish and Kip wondered if he thought it seedy and run-down. He made no comment but got out to come round her side of the car.

'Thanks for the lift,' she said stiffly as he held open the door.

He acknowledged her gratitude with a nod, then said, 'I'll let you know what I intend doing.'

'About what?'

'Your assignment... I can't just let it go.'

Kip's anger came back full force. He still thought that she'd cheated. He could give her a lift home, talk pleasantly to her, even suggest that she could be a companion to his daughter, yet he still thought her a cheat.

'Wait here!' she barked at him, forgetting their respective positions, then quickly mounted the staircase to her apartment.

It took time to open the door, as it had more than one security lock. She glanced down. He was waiting by the foot of the steps.

She went straight for the recorder by her bed. It was a good machine—the only piece of high-tech equipment she owned. She'd bought it to record and play back lectures rather than take notes, but had quickly realised that it wasn't going to make up for her reading and writing deficiencies. She emptied the machine and made for the door.

She found him at the top of the steps and gave a little start

of fright before recovering sufficiently to shove the tape in
his hand. 'Here.'

He took it, lifting a questioning brow in her direction.

She gave no explanation, but, pulling shut her door, said,
'I have to go to work.'

Whit didn't try to stop her but watched as she ran down
the stairs and turned the corner to the pizza parlour. He realised what the tape was. He went down to his car and listened
to it as he drove home.

It wasn't a very sophisticated recording but it was clearly
her voice. It was surprisingly soft, rising and falling with just
the suggestion of a regional accent. It was also her words,
before they'd been transcribed by a typist and given to him.
He'd made one rather large mistake.

'Found yourself a boyfriend?' Sam asked her halfway
through her night's work.

'No. Why?' Kip wondered if he'd seen Whit Delaney drop
her off.

'Someone's just phoned and asked to speak to you,' Sam
relayed.

Kip pulled a face. Who else but Whit Delaney? She didn't
want to speak to him.

'I told him you were working and not to call on my time,'
Sam added, much to her relief, and handed her two plates
over the serving counter. 'A Neapolitan and Hawaiian for
table six.'

For once Kip was grateful for Sam's grumpiness. Another
boss might have called her to the phone. But not Sam. He
paid her and the other waitresses by the second.

Kip did the rest of her shift on remote control, and if she
kept thinking about Whit Delaney it was entirely involuntary.

'I'll let you off early,' Sam announced when their last customer had departed and she'd cleaned all the tables.

'Early' was five minutes, but it was a first, so Kip dutifully
noted it with, 'Thanks, Sam.'

'He's waiting outside—' Sam nodded towards the street
'—your caller.'

'What?' Kip stared at him blankly.

'The guy that phoned,' Sam said, deadpan. 'He wanted to know when your shift ended. Said to tell you he'd be out front.'

'That was ages ago,' Kip pointed out.

Sam lifted his shoulders in an offhand gesture. 'I wasn't having you mooning about him through the whole shift.'

'He's not a boyfriend,' Kip stated for a second time.

'And the pope's not a Catholic.' Sam gave her one of his rare, brief smiles. 'Go on, before he gets tired of waiting.'

Rather than argue, Kip hung up her apron, then went to the front door. She'd been serving tables right by the window all night and had seen no one lurking about. Perhaps Sam had got it wrong.

She walked out onto the street and, seeing no car, quickly turned up her alleyway. There, parked as it had been earlier, was his Jaguar.

She was quick, heading stealthily up the staircase, but not quick enough. He spotted her before she could unlock her door and get inside.

'Kipling—' he got out of his car '—wait up.'

Kip intended to ignore him, but she had forgotten about the series of locks on her door. She was fiddling with one that could be awkward when he joined her on the top step.

'I tried phoning but your boss refused to let you talk,' he explained unnecessarily.

She found herself defending Sam. 'I'm there to work, not talk.'

'That's exactly what he said. You're not related, are you?' he enquired drily.

'No.' Kip pulled a face, then went back to struggling with the lock. The key required two turns one way, a click, then one turn the other. It also required a degree of calmness that had deserted her.

She would have screamed if he'd offered to do it for her. She hated men who regarded women as incompetent and took over. But he didn't offer so she decided that he was no gentleman.

'May I come in?' he asked when she finally turned the key in the lock.

'It's late,' she replied.

'Just give me a chance.' He put a foot in the door before she could close it.

'A chance?' She turned to look at him with suspicion.

'To apologise.' His expression told her that he was serious.

Kip still looked at him doubtfully, and it was with reluctance that she agreed, 'OK; come in.'

She switched on the light and he followed her in. It wasn't a big apartment. The living room served as a bedroom and kitchen. Only the toilet and shower were separate.

The sofa bed was still folded out, with a tangle of sheets and duvet. The small table had the remains of breakfast on it. The room looked a tip and Kip was surprised into feeling shame. Normally she didn't care what state her apartment was in.

She resisted the temptation to tidy up or excuse the mess. She watched him glance round and half anticipated some derogatory remark.

Instead he gave a half-smile and said, 'I think I've found a soul mate.'

'Pardon?' Kip wasn't sure that she understood.

'I'm not the tidiest of people either,' he explained as she cleared a chair of clean washing so that he could sit. 'Still, I'd say you have the edge on me.'

'I haven't time,' Kip said defensively.

'No, I don't suppose you have,' he conceded levelly, taking the seat he'd been offered. 'How many nights do you work downstairs?'

'Six,' she said briefly, remaining on her feet.

'And how often do you train?' he added.

She shrugged before listing, 'In the mornings, as you know. Most lunchtimes—three with Mr Scott. Saturdays when there isn't a meet. Sunday afternoons with Mr Scott.'

'That sounds a lot,' he commented.

She shook her head. 'Not if you're serious about it.'

'I suppose,' he agreed. 'But it can't leave a lot of time over.'

Kip's lips thinned. 'For studying, you mean?'

'Actually, no,' he replied. 'I wasn't thinking about your studies so much as leisure time.'

Leisure time? Kip wondered if he was being facetious.

But no, he went on to ask, 'What do you do when you're not training, working or studying?'

'I sleep,' she answered briefly.

Whit Delaney laughed for a moment before he realised that she was being literal, then a frown settled between his brows. He glanced from the sofa bed, left ready for reoccupation, to the shelves empty of anything but textbooks. There were no photographs, no ornaments, nothing that suggested a personal life.

Kip followed his gaze and saw the place through his eyes. She really hadn't made much effort. She pushed a bag of washing under her bed before asking him, 'Why have you come?'

He got to the point of his visit. 'I listened to the tape. I realised I'd made a mistake. I can't tell you how sorry I am.' He sounded sincere.

Kip unbent a little. 'It doesn't matter.' She shrugged, meaning to let him off the hook.

'Yes, it does.' Whit understood what damage he'd done and wanted to repair it. 'You took the time and trouble to come up with a decent essay and I threw it back in your face. It just wasn't what I expected.'

Kip knew that. She knew what he'd expected. Very little. It was what teachers had always expected of her.

'I'm dyslexic!' she threw back. 'I'm not stupid!'

'No,' he agreed, 'but perhaps I am. If I'd studied the essay I would have known it was your work. The words on the page were you—the tone, the ideas, everything.' He ran on, 'I should have known without having to listen to a tape.'

Kip stared at him warily. What did he mean—the words were her? He didn't know her. He couldn't. She was a secret—a secret even to herself.

'That's why it was so original,' he continued. 'Most students simply read what other critics have written on a play, then regurgitate on paper. You didn't do that.'

His tone was clearly one of admiration, but Kip felt as uncomfortable with praise as she did with any kind of interest in her.

'I didn't,' she returned drily, 'because I couldn't. I can't read, remember?'

'But you can listen.' He ignored her tough response and went on, 'You listened a damn sight better than most of the others read, and you understood.'

'Not all of it.' Kip really wasn't sure if she liked the way this conversation was going. She was used to being regarded as a dunce. It seemed easier, at this stage, to stick with the role she'd been given.

'No one understands all of it,' he countered. 'You're just a hell of a lot closer than most people. The question is, what are we going to do about it?'

'About what?' Kip asked warily.

'The fact that you have an IQ that outstrips your reading age by miles,' he stated, intentionally blunt.

Kip stared at him, immune to any compliment. No one knew that fact better than she did. She'd lived with it for years.

At one time she had raged against it—the frustration of struggling to read the most basic books, struggling to express the ideas buzzing about in her head. But the rage had burnt itself out long since and she had lost interest in the ideas, or at least in conveying them to the rest of the world. She didn't need someone coming along breaking through layers of indifference.

She wasn't grateful. She was angry.

'Well, we could wave a magic wand,' she suggested, 'or wish on a star, or how about writing to Santa...? No, on second thoughts, scrub the last. He could never decipher my handwriting.'

The sarcasm wasn't lost on Whit. He asked himself what

he was doing here. Far from being pleased with his interest, she plainly resented it. But what had he expected?

Gratitude, he supposed. More fool him, then, to imagine that this girl would express such. She was more likely to tell him where to shove his patronage, and who could blame her?

The wisest course would be to get the hell out of a female student's room and stop playing Mr Chips. But some other, stronger impulse made him remain where he was.

'You're right.' He tried again. 'There's no easy solution. Maybe there's no solution, period, but you have to at least try.'

'Why?' she countered simply.

Why? Whit looked for an answer that might appeal to her. She stared back at him with those sharp green eyes that saw so much—too much, perhaps—and realised that there was no carrot he could dangle that would be worth a damn to this girl. So he opted for the stick.

'Because if you don't,' he told her simply, 'I'll go to the dean and recommend your immediate exclusion from Radford.'

Kip stared at him in disbelief. He wouldn't do that. She might not know much about this man, but she knew enough. He wouldn't do that.

'You're bluffing,' she muttered sullenly.

Whit wasn't sure whether he was bluffing or not, but he'd played poker in his time. He caught her eyes with his and looked at her, and went on doing so until she was the one to look away.

'Why are you doing this?' she demanded, angry again.

Whit didn't rightly know. He'd always believed that people shouldn't be coerced into learning, but that was exactly what he was doing with Kip Wilson.

'Someone has to,' he answered her, and, before she could contradict him, ran on, 'But, in point of fact, it won't be me.'

'What won't?' Kip had lost her thread.

'Who'll be giving you extra tuition,' he stated matter-of-factly. 'It'll be my father.'

Proud, Kip countered, 'I have no money for tuition.'

'I guessed that.' Whit's gaze ranged round her apartment. No one would live in this place from choice. Not even this girl. 'It's what you'd call a reciprocal arrangement. You need tutoring. My father needs to tutor. It's his life, teaching, but he can't come back till he's recovered further. He needs a project.'

And presumably she was it, Kip concluded, scowling. 'Have you asked your father?'

'A couple of weeks back,' he confirmed, 'and he's all for it. He's already consulted the Dyslexia Foundation for technical advice on teaching methods... There's nothing my father likes better than a challenge.'

'I feel like Everest,' Kip muttered in flippant reply.

He smiled a little before saying, 'So that's agreed.'

'No!' Kip didn't remember agreeing to anything. 'I can't... Even if I wanted to, I just don't have the time.'

He'd obviously anticipated the problem. 'I'll let you out of my tutorial groups.'

'You will?' she muttered in disbelief.

'Why not?' He shrugged in response. 'It's not as if you ever take part or listen to what's going on.'

Kip blushed with guilt. 'It's nothing personal,' she murmured back. 'I've never liked school.'

'Maybe it was the school you attended,' he suggested.

Kip laughed shortly. 'The ten.'

It took Whit a moment to understand. 'You went to ten different schools?'

Kip nodded. 'I wasn't expelled or anything,' she said, before he could suggest it. 'We just moved around a lot.'

'"We"?' he picked up. 'How many of you were there?'

'Only me and my dad,' she related. 'My mother died when I was three.'

'And he brought you up?' Whit concluded.

'You could call it that,' Kip muttered under her breath.

He still caught it, raising a curious brow. 'What would you call it?'

Kip, however, was already regretting giving anything away. She had once admitted to a teacher that her father drank too much. She had hastily recanted when a social worker had descended on them.

'Nothing.' She shook her head in dismissal.

But he pursued the subject, saying, 'I could do with the advice. I'm a single father myself.'

Kip doubted it was the same thing and felt the impulse to shock. 'All right. When you get pissed, make sure there's someone other than your kid to put you to bed.'

Whit didn't laugh, although he thought for a moment that it was some kind of joke. Her face told him that it wasn't. If anything, it was a warning to back off.

Instead he asked, 'Do you still see him?'

'My father?' Kip replied, 'No, he died.'

'I'm sorry.' Whit knew that the words were inadequate.

She rejected his sympathy, stating matter-of-factly, 'It was a relief…for him, anyway.'

It hadn't been for Kip. She had hated her father and loved him in equal measure. She had been ashamed for him every time he got drunk and stupid and cried. But he had died sober and sad and oddly brave, and it had been no relief.

Tears welled up in her eyes but she turned away before Whit Delaney could see them. She hated pity. She'd seen too much of it when people looked at her father.

Whit rose and went to where she stood by the window. 'You must miss him,' he said quietly.

He meant to be kind but it just made Kip angry. What did he know?

'Why must I miss him?' she demanded. 'Because it's normal? Obligatory? Or just the right thing to say?'

God, she was difficult! Whit felt his own emotions conflicting wildly. How could he want both to protect and hurt her at one and the same time?

He put a hand on her shoulder and she flinched from his touch. He should have left then. Instead he caught her by the arm and pulled her round.

'Let me go!' she spat at him, but he ignored her.

'At least look at a person,' he ground out, 'when you're telling them to go to hell!'

'All right!' Kip raised her head to his, and green eyes clashed with blue. She meant to tell him just that—to go to hell, get lost, leave her alone. But she hesitated and something changed as they went on staring at each other. Something made her forget the words, forget the anger. Something made her heart suddenly beat too hard.

For Whit it was an urge—a crazy, inexplicable urge. He gave way to it before he could even analyse it. He drew her into his arms and she cried out, startled, but his mouth was already on hers.

Kip had been kissed before—clumsy kisses from clumsy boys—but never like this. His lips moved on hers, hard, possessive, demanding—above all, knowing. Knowing how to make her breath stop and her senses spin. Knowing how to make her want to open her lips and give way to the rush of pleasure, the wave of desire.

For Whit the urge turned into full-scale insanity when he felt her willing response. It had been so long since he'd felt it—passion, pure passion, not cultivated or calculated, but a living thing rapidly running out of control.

He kissed her harder, began to touch her, his hands sliding over her back, to her hips, her thighs—strong arms lifting her, bodies sliding, entwining, falling onto the bed.

It was all new to Kip, but it felt as natural as breathing. There were no wrongs or rights in her head, just the sound of her heartbeat, loud and strong, drowning out thought. It was like a race—limbs gliding, blood rushing, skin slick with sweat. Like a race, except for once she was running with someone else and there was no loneliness, no despair.

He should have stopped himself. Whit knew it then. He knew it later. He tried. He took his mouth from hers and made himself look at her, made himself remember that this was a girl, not a woman; this was one of his students, someone he barely knew. He looked down at her and saw how young she was, but it didn't change anything. Her eyes were green fire and her mouth was soft and moist with promise. He still wanted her.

She should have stopped him. Whit told himself that later

too. When he pushed aside her clothing to touch her damp, sweet flesh, she should have stopped him, not moaned with the pleasure he gave her. Not made him want to give her more. Not made him want to touch her everywhere, then cover her body with his and take what she seemed so willing to offer. She should have cried out at the beginning, not the end, when it was too late and the gift had been given—a gift he didn't want.

It hurt. Kip hadn't expected it to. She hadn't been ready, and the pain startled her. Worse, it brought her back to reality. He lifted his head from hers and she saw a stranger, and stared at him in horror.

Whit felt her body shudder in repudiation and reacted with his own kind of horror. He rolled off her and sat on the edge of the bed. He wanted to get up, walk out the door and keep walking. He pulled on his discarded clothing, in a rage of shame and frustration, but he didn't follow his instincts this time.

Kip wished he would go. Just get up and go, leave her to make sense of what she'd just done. In twenty-one years she'd never had a boyfriend, never wanted one, though the offers had been there. This man, this stranger, had touched her and she'd gone to bed with him without even stopping to think about it.

'I didn't realise,' he said, when he eventually turned to look at her.

Kip understood what he meant but she said nothing in reply. She just clutched the duvet to her chin.

Whit looked at the huge green eyes on him and his guilt registered ten on the Richter scale. What was wrong with him? She was just a kid.

He put out a hand to touch her. She flinched from it. 'Go away, please,' she said in a small, tight voice.

'I can't. Not like this.' Whit felt a protective urge once more, even if it was singularly inappropriate. He'd just joined the list of people who'd messed up this girl.

Kip saw the anxious look on his face but read it as concern for himself. 'Don't worry. I won't tell anyone.'

'I don't care about that.' Whit ran a distracted hand through his hair. 'You can tell the world I'm a bastard if you like. I won't dispute it. I just don't know why I—' Whit broke off, feeling that any excuses for his behaviour would make things worse.

He hadn't reckoned on the girl's honesty. 'It was my fault. I should have stopped you. I didn't.' She summed up the situation in emotionless tones. 'Could you go now?'

She sounded so cool, so in control. Her eyes were dry, her face a mask. Whit wondered if she ever felt real emotion. He had just taken her virginity but he hadn't reached her. Perhaps no one ever would.

He got up from the bed and picked up his jacket and left.

Kip stared at the door as it closed behind him. Only then did the pain and shame and loneliness leak out of her. Only then did the tears slip silently down her face like rain on a window-pane.

CHAPTER FOUR

'Yes?' Hostile eyes were trained on Kip.

'Is this Professor Delaney's house?' Kip asked, checking the piece of paper with his address.

'It might be.' An elderly woman looked her up and down. 'You're not another one, are you?'

'Another what?' Kip asked blankly.

'Babysitter.' Alice Novak sniffed at the word. 'More trouble than they're worth, if you ask me.'

'I'm not a babysitter,' Kip denied. 'I'm here to see Professor Delaney senior. Professor Delaney sent me.'

The housekeeper still looked suspicious, as if she thought that Kip might be some kind of con artist. Kip could have shown her the letter in her hand, but it didn't seem a terribly good idea. Whit Delaney hadn't wasted too many words:

Dear Kipling,
Should you wish to report me to the college authorities, that is your right. My father will still expect you for tuition, concurrent with your literature tutorials.
Regards,
Whit Delaney.

Brief and to the point as it was, Kip hadn't taken overlong to decipher it—or read between the lines. She had a choice. She could kick up a fuss and accuse him of taking advantage of her, or she could keep her mouth shut, save them both the embarrassment and go along and see his father.

It wasn't much of a choice, which was why she was here,

at 10 Washington Avenue, getting grief from some sourpuss of a housekeeper.

'Look, if there's a problem—' she shrugged '—I'll go away. But you'd better tell him I've been here.'

So saying, Kip went back down the steps.

Alice Novak called out, 'Hold up, girl! I didn't say there was a problem, did I?'

Kip halted at the bottom, half wishing that the housekeeper had let her go. She wasn't sure if she wanted to set foot in Whit Delaney's house, even if he wasn't there.

'If Professor Delaney's expecting you, you'd better come in.' The woman held the door open for her.

Reluctantly Kip reclimbed the steps and entered the house.

'Wait here.' Alice Novak hadn't totally got over her mistrust. 'I'll find the professor.'

Kip was left in the hall. She glanced round. There was a staircase leading to the first floor and a room off each side of the hall. The one on the right was furnished in a shabby but comfortable style—old-fashioned, like a film set from the forties or fifties. The other was a study or library, lined from floor to ceiling with books.

The housekeeper returned from the back of the house with Professor Alex Delaney.

'Ah, Kipling, how nice to see you.' His smile was welcoming.

Kip smiled back. She'd always liked this man. He hadn't intruded into her privacy.

'You look well,' she said quite genuinely. The professor looked better than he had when she'd last seen him, just before his heart attack.

'Thank you; I feel it,' he confirmed, and, indicating the room on the left, said, 'Will we go into my study and get down to business?'

Kip nodded, her tension slipping away. She'd forgotten what an easy man Delaney senior was—unlike his son. She followed him into the book-lined room and sat on a chair by the desk.

'Do you think we might have some coffee, Alice?' Alex Delaney added to the housekeeper hovering in the doorway.

'I suppose,' she agreed grudgingly. 'Just don't go tiring yourself out.'

The words were directed at the professor, but it was Kip who received the warning look.

'Don't mind Alice,' the professor reassured Kip with a smile. 'She likes treating me like an invalid. She thinks fifteen years of working for me gives her the right to be bossy. And—who knows?—perhaps it does.'

Kip was still worried. Maybe the housekeeper had reason to fuss. It wasn't many weeks since Alex Delaney had had a heart attack.

'Professor,' she began tentatively, 'you don't have to do this. I mean, I'm not sure there's much point. I don't think I'll ever be able to read or write…not properly, anyway. And I don't want to waste your time—'

'Time?' The professor gave a dry chuckle. 'Right at the moment that's all I've got. Time, and nothing to do with it but sit and watch the world go by… So let's not worry about *my* time when it's really yours that's at issue.'

'Mine?' she queried.

'Yours.' He nodded. 'For would I not be right in thinking that you'd sooner be training than studying?'

It was true, Kip supposed. She'd been reluctant to come. But now she was here it seemed important to stay.

She shook her head and replied simply, 'I can't read. I want to learn.'

The professor smiled slightly. 'Well, I'd say you're already part way to solving that problem.'

'I am?' Kip didn't see how.

'Admitting a problem,' he went on, 'is half the solution. Like drunks saying "I am an alcoholic".'

It was a bad choice. Kip's eyes darkened as she wondered if Whit Delaney had blabbed about her father.

'The comparison wasn't meant to offend,' his father assured quickly when he saw her expression.

No, Kip realised, Whit hadn't told him. She was the one

being over-sensitive. And what the professor had said was true enough. Her father had never solved his problem because he had never admitted it.

'Sorry,' Kip responded, then drily added, 'My name's Kip Wilson, and I'm a dyslexic.'

He chuckled at her somewhat dark humour. 'Well, let's see what we can do to help.'

Nothing, Kip imagined, but she didn't say so. Cynicism seemed wrong in the face of his confidence as he proceeded to explain his work plan.

He had already done much preparation, having read books on dyslexia and illiteracy. He spent the first tuition hour giving her a battery of tests so that he could identify the severity of her problem and the best approach to take. There was no absolute cure for dyslexia but it seemed there were various tricks that could be used to overcome the handicap.

Kip didn't end the hour feeling especially hopeful, but the time passed quickly and Alex Delaney had enough enthusiasm for both of them.

'I'll see you Wednesday,' he said at the end of the lesson. 'Unless, of course, you decide to opt back into my son's classes.'

'No, I'll come to you,' Kip replied hastily.

The older man gave a dry laugh. 'I take it Whit—my son's been giving you a hard time.'

'That's one word for it.' Kip could think of others, but she didn't want to shock this kind old man.

'Attitude incompatibility,' he added. 'That's what my son called it.'

Had that been before or after they'd gone to bed together? Kip wondered. Either, she supposed. Going to bed hadn't made them more compatible. Just crazier.

'Really?' Kip asked tightly, and Alex Delaney studied her for a moment but didn't comment.

'Can you show yourself out?' he asked instead.

'Sure,' she agreed, already halfway to the hall before she turned to say, 'Thanks, Professor.'

'No thanks needed. Just come back.' He smiled.

Kip nodded, intending to.

As she let herself out she met the housekeeper on the door-step. Beside her stood a little girl clutching a lunch-pail. Presumably this was Abby Delaney, back from school.

'Is the professor all right?' the woman demanded of Kip.

'Yes, fine,' Kip assured her, and offered a conciliatory, 'Thanks for the coffee.'

'It was no trouble.' Alice unbent slightly.

'You're not *another* new babysitter, are you?' her small companion piped up.

'Hush, child,' Alice instructed her smartly.

To no effect, as the little girl continued, 'Because you won't last. I've got through three already. The first cackled like a hen, and the second was about as much fun as getting a tooth pulled. As for this week's—Silly Stacey—'

'Stacey is still employed, as far as I know,' Alice Novak cut in, 'so hold your tongue, Abigail Delaney, and get into the house.'

But Abigail Delaney was incorrigible, directing at Kip, 'So who are you?'

'My name's Kip Wilson,' she answered the girl. 'I'm a student of your grandfather's.'

'And my dad's?'

'Yes.'

'Are you the poor thing—the one that can't read properly?' the little girl enquired.

'*Abigail Delaney!*' the housekeeper exclaimed in fury.

Kip felt angry too—angry that the Delaney men would discuss her in front of this precocious child.

'Yes,' she retorted, 'and you must be the rude one—the one who has no manners.'

It was Abigail's turn to be shocked. Her little face screwed up, then went beetroot.

Kip didn't wait to see her stamp her foot. She felt no triumph in upsetting the child. She might be a brat but she was only repeating what she'd overheard.

Kip had always detested pity and the word 'poor' smacked of it. Was that how Whit Delaney saw her? A 'poor thing'?

Well, she wasn't going back to the Delaney household to be patronised by the inhabitants—precocious children included.

Leave it alone. That was what Whit told himself when he returned from college to discover that his daughter was holed up in her bedroom, refusing to come down.

He sent Stacey home because she had no child to look after, then listened to Alice Novak's version of events. Apparently Abigail had been rude to the English girl and the girl had told her so. Alice had no problem with that. It was, after all, the truth. Unfortunately Abigail didn't like hearing home truths and had stamped off upstairs.

'Did you say it?' he enquired of Abby, repeating the words that Alice Novak had relayed to him.

'Might of.' Abby's face was a picture of sullenness.

'Might have,' he corrected automatically.

'It's only what Gramps said,' she ran on, 'when you asked him to teach her. He said he would do it willingly because "it's a poor thing, not being able to read properly".' This time Abigail quoted exactly, her eyes all innocence.

Whit wasn't fooled. 'But that's not what you said to her, was it?'

'It was nearly,' Abby claimed. 'I can't help it if she misunderstood.'

'Yes, you can,' her father responded heavily. 'You know and I know you said it to be hurtful. What I don't know is why you'd want to hurt someone you don't even know.'

Abigail shrugged, then, as her father sat there watching her, looked sheepish before admitting, 'I thought she was a new babysitter, but she said she wasn't so I felt disappointed.'

'What?' Whit didn't follow. 'You don't like babysitters.'

'I don't like the other ones,' Abigail confirmed, 'but she looked different. She looked as though she wouldn't giggle all the time or ask me stupid questions or pretend to care about me just to make a fast buck.'

'A fast buck?' Mentally, Whit raised his eyebrows. 'What have you been watching?'

'Nothing,' Abby replied. 'I read it.'

'Well, you shouldn't be reading trash,' he countered.

Abby smiled wickedly. 'I read it in one of your books. *Cold Blood.*' She named his most recently published thriller.

Whit blanched. 'How much did you read?'

'Just a few pages...' she said dismissively. 'I didn't get to any of the sexy bits.'

Whit groaned inwardly. Sometimes he was proud of having the smartest kid on the block. At others it seemed like a curse.

'Well, I repeat, you shouldn't be reading trash,' he said, having no special sensitivity regarding his own work. He wrote books full of suspense and humour. He didn't write masterpieces.

Abigail laughed up at him. Somehow, she'd insinuated herself onto his knee. So much for being firm with her.

'Look, Abby—' he tried again '—you mustn't put people down just because you're feeling bad. How do you think Kipling Wilson felt when you said she couldn't read properly?'

Abby thought for a moment before remarking, 'She was angry, but she got her own back. She said I was rude.'

'You are,' her father accused her in reply.

'I suppose,' Abby grudgingly admitted, then switched to asking, 'Has Stacey gone?'

He nodded. 'And we'll be lucky if she comes back too.'

Abby's face brightened at the prospect of being *un*lucky. 'Then we could ask the other girl to babysit.'

'The other girl?' he echoed. 'You mean Kipling Wilson?'

Abby nodded.

Whit was surprised. Why would she want the English girl? Unless, of course, she recognised a soul mate. Disturbing thought. He certainly didn't want Abby turning out like Kip Wilson.

'Miss Wilson—' he tried distancing himself from the blasted girl '—has an after-college job.'

'Doing what?' Abby enquired.

'None of your business.' Whit didn't want to give his

daughter future ammunition—always assuming that Kip returned for more tuition from his father.

Leave it alone. He told himself the same thing several times over dinner with his father. But, at nine, he slung on a jacket and drove to the other side of town.

When he walked into the pizza parlour she looked horrified. She scurried away before he could come near. He walked up to the serving hatch and waited for the man working at the pizza ovens to notice him.

'Problem, buddy?' Sam didn't waste too much courtesy on his clientele.

'I'd like to talk to Kipling if that's possible,' Whit said in level tones.

'*Kipling?*' Sam pulled a face at the full version of Kip's name, before saying, 'I don't like my waitresses associating during working hours.'

'I'm her literature professor.' Whit tried using his position.

Sam was deeply unimpressed. 'So?' He shrugged. 'School's out, buddy.'

'True—' Whit didn't give him an argument '—and I know she's working, so I'll pay for her time.'

Sam's eyes narrowed on him in suspicion.

Whit didn't blame him. Literature professors didn't normally pursue their students and offer to buy their time. What was he doing here? She was becoming an obsession.

Still, Sam decided in his favour. 'You buy a pizza, you talk to the waitress. OK, buddy?'

'Yeah, fine.' Whit had already eaten but he took Sam's advice and walked over to a table.

She was serving a couple of tables away. She passed him *en route* to the kitchen, her face taut, but she didn't acknowledge him.

'Yes?' A redhead with purple fingernails stood before him, waiting to take his order. He hadn't realised that there were two of them.

'Nothing personal,' he told her, 'but could I have the other waitress?'

'Nothing personal, mister—' she smiled broadly '—but she's just offered to swap me two loud-mouth drunks for you, and I sure ain't complaining.'

Whit followed the redhead's gaze to the back of the parlour, where Kip Wilson was taking the order of a couple of middle-aged men. Whit couldn't hear what was being said but he could tell that the men were giving her a hard time.

'Relax, bud.' His waitress blocked his way when he would have gone to Kip. 'The kid can handle those two easy, and she ain't gonna thank you for interfering... So what'll it be?' she stuck the menu in front of his face.

'Anything,' he said dismissively, 'and coffee.'

'Chef's special?' she suggested.

'Great.' Whit didn't care. His eyes had returned to the table with the drunks but Kip had disappeared.

The redhead followed his gaze. 'Tell you what, mister— when your pizza's ready, I'll make sure I'm unavailable. OK?'

'Thanks.' Whit was grateful.

Ten minutes later he heard Sam call, 'Rhea, table five,' then repeat it a couple of times, before shouting, 'Kip, get this, will you?'

He was waiting. He kept his eyes fixed on the table till she was right up close. She tried to slap the pizza on the table and run. His hand shot out and he grabbed her wrist.

'Let me go!' she spat at him, trying and failing to twist free.

He held her fast. 'Not until I've had my say.'

'You'll get me fired,' she cried furiously.

'Then keep your voice down,' he suggested, his own quiet and controlled. 'We can talk now or we can talk later... Only I don't think later would be too wise, do you?' he added.

They both remembered what had happened the last time they'd been alone together. Her eyes narrowed like a fox's, quick and cunning, but her mouth was like a child's, soft and trembling.

Whit asked himself once more what he was doing. She

was both dangerous and vulnerable—a fatal combination. He didn't need this grief.

'Why can't you leave me alone?' She asked the question for him.

Whit wished that he knew the answer. He'd promised himself to keep away. He would keep away after this.

'I'm sorry about Abby...what she said,' he told her straight.

'She was only repeating what you told her,' she accused him.

He shook his head. 'Do you really believe I'd discuss my students with my eight-year-old daughter? She eavesdropped, then misquoted,' he related briefly.

Kip believed him, but it didn't make her feel any more kindly disposed towards him. 'Is that it? Can I go now?' She looked pointedly at the long fingers holding her wrist.

He didn't release her. 'After you promise you'll continue tuition with my father.'

Kip frowned. Why was he bothering? Guilt? Fear of exposure? What?

'I'll make sure Abby stays out of your way,' he added.

She answered the thoughts in her head, saying, 'I'm not going to tell anybody about...about last week, so you can stop worrying.'

'I'm not worrying about that,' he claimed. 'Tell whoever you like. I'll live with it.'

He sounded convincing, as if he didn't care. Perhaps he didn't. After all, it might enhance his reputation. It just wouldn't do much for hers.

'You think *I'd* want anyone to know?' she retorted.

Her eyes were cold now, like her heart. Whit shook his head. 'I don't know what to think. I'm not sure I understand myself what happened between us.'

Kip's face coloured. She didn't really understand either, but she didn't want to talk about it.

'I'll carry on with the tuition,' she stated flatly.

He was surprised by the sudden capitulation. 'Good. My

father's certain he can help you. He says you have an extremely high IQ.'

'Yeah, I'm Einstein.' Kip dismissed the compliment, assuming that it was false. 'That's why I'm serving pizzas for a living... Speaking of which, yours is getting cold,' she added, and, with this reminder of her current position, finally slipped from his grip.

Whit let her go. He'd done what he'd come to do. She'd agreed to keep working with his father. There was no reason to hang around longer.

But he did. He watched her serve a bowling crowd. She did it deftly, impersonally, oblivious to the younger men trying to shoot her a line.

He remembered her saying that she didn't date. He could believe it. She seemed to have little desire or need for company. Hard-hearted, hard-headed, she seemed to have no feelings at all. Yet she had been so soft, so warm in his arms, and he had felt... What had he felt?

He couldn't remember. He didn't want to remember. Too long without a woman—that was his trouble. He disliked sleeping with women he didn't know well, so he slept with no one in between relationships, and his last relationship had been nine months ago. A pleasant, uncomplicated affair with a publishing assistant in New York, it had ended on good terms when he had moved to Maine.

Maybe he needed someone new, but it certainly wasn't Kip Wilson. She had 'trouble' tattooed across her forehead in big letters. It was only in the dingy light of her apartment that he'd missed it.

He pushed the pizza away untouched and threw a fifty-dollar bill down on the table before leaving.

Kip watched him go. She saw the fifty. The large tip from it would have been extremely useful but she let Rhea claim it. She didn't need his guilt money.

Kip carried on with the tuition quite willingly. She liked and admired the older professor. He was a wise and gentle man. He was also an inspiring teacher. He believed in her, and, in doing so, reached Kip in ways that others had failed. First he surprised her by stating that she was not, in fact, dyslexic. She had been given that label by a teacher and it had been preferable to 'thick'. The professor's battery of tests, however, refuted it.

At first Kip was less than overjoyed. Dyslexia was a recognised condition and explained her illiteracy. Now she wondered if she was just plain incapable. But the professor told her that the tests indicated a high IQ, and, whatever the reason for her problem, it could surely be eradicated.

His confidence was infectious and Kip worked hard for him—harder than she ever had before—so that within a matter of weeks the improvement in her reading and written work was quite phenomenal.

'We need more time together,' the professor said one afternoon as they came to the end of the tuition hour. 'How about this Saturday? You don't have an athletics meeting, do you?'

'Not a meeting, no.' It was almost December and the New England winter had already taken hold. The athletics season was over. Bill Scott had suggested that she should give herself a break and recharge her batteries, but Kip still trained on a daily basis.

Alex Delaney sensed her reluctance, smiling as he said, 'Never mind. Whit said you'd have other things to do at the weekend.'

'Did he?' Kip wondered out loud, and some devil in her made her say, 'He's wrong. I can come if you like.'

'Great.' The older man beamed widely. 'Come for lunch and we'll work through the afternoon.'

'I…no…' Kip regretted her acceptance. 'I can't. I'm on a special diet,' she lied quickly, 'for fitness.'

'No problem.' He continued to smile affably. 'Mrs Novak can cook something specific.'

'I don't want to be any trouble.' Kip knew that Alice Novak wouldn't be too happy about catering for her. Although the housekeeper had been pleasant enough since their first meeting, she wasn't backward about airing her opinions on students in general.

'It's no trouble, and I'd enjoy the company,' the professor assured her. 'My son's going to New York for the weekend and little Abby's going to a friend's house.'

'I...' Kip had run out of excuses, and with Whit Delaney not in attendance would lunch be so awful? 'All right, thanks.'

'Let's find Alice and you can tell her about your dietary requirements. She's probably in the kitchen.' He got up from his chair and led the way through the hall to the back of the house.

Kip followed reluctantly, wondering how she could take back her lie.

The kitchen was like the rest of the Delaney house—large, old-fashioned and homely. Alice was kneading dough at the table.

'I've invited Kipling for lunch on Saturday,' Alex Delaney announced, 'if that's all right.'

Alice looked surprised but not especially annoyed. 'I can cook for two as easily as one, Professor.'

'Yes, well, there's a problem—' he continued with an apologetic air.

Kip stepped in smartly. 'I'm allergic to chilli powder,' she stated, with a degree of truth this time.

'Never use it.' Alice snorted at the idea. 'Buy the right meat at the market and you don't need to disguise its taste.'

'I can eat just about anything else,' Kip added helpfully, ignoring the professor's puzzled look.

'Good, because I can't stand faddy eaters,' Alice declared bluntly, then, glancing towards the kitchen clock, added, 'Which reminds me, I'd better go and fetch her ladyship.'

She went to get her coat off the kitchen door while the professor explained to Kip, '"Her ladyship" is my grand-daughter, Abby. Alice and Abby have what you might call a love-hate relationship.'

'Tsk!' Alice Novak made the dismissive sound before muttering, 'Well, she can't twist *me* around her little finger, that's for sure.'

Alex Delaney shook his head but didn't argue with the housekeeper. It was obviously a familiar refrain, and Alice Novak was allowed to air her views more freely than most employees.

Her only concession to her position was her rider of, 'Still, far be it from me to express an opinion.'

This drew a smile of irony to the older man's lips and, for once, Kip was reminded of his son. They didn't look much like each other but they had similar expressions. The big difference was personality. Delaney senior was a decent, straightforward, likeable man. His son had none of these qualities.

'You walking my way?' Alice Novak asked when they found themselves on the pavement outside.

Kip nodded and fell in step beside her.

'You from London, England?' the housekeeper added as they walked.

Kip shook her head and volunteered, 'Manchester.'

''Bout the same thing.' Alice viewed England as being the equivalent of an American state. '*She* was English—Abby's mother.'

'Did you know her?' Kip was curious despite herself.

'Met her once or twice,' Alice confirmed. 'Very the-a-tri-cal,' she declared in damning tones, 'but then I suppose she was meant to be. Being a movie star and all.'

'Wh—? Professor Delaney was married to a movie star?' Kip repeated this wildly unlikely information.

Alice Novak nodded. 'Starred in one of his films.'

'*His films?*' Kip began to wonder if the housekeeper might be a compulsive liar. 'He directs films?'

'Lord, no!' Alice dismissed, with a snort. 'They make films of the books he writes. You'd better keep quiet about that, though. He doesn't like to advertise the fact.'

'I'm not really interested.' Kip suspected that it was all a fantasy of the housekeeper.

'You may not be—' Alice Novak sniffed '—but you can bet your bottom dollar that other girl will be. That Tracy, or whatever she calls herself.'

'Stacey,' Kip corrected her.

'Thinks she's God's gift, that one,' Alice Novak ran on. 'Has a notion for the professor too, if you ask me.'

'Which one?' Kip said, tongue-in-cheek.

'Whitman, of course!' Alice Novak looked askance at her. 'Though it's just as disgusting. A girl of her age chasing a man of his... Still, he's not the type to take advantage.'

This time Kip kept any cynical thoughts to herself. She hadn't decided what 'type' Whit Delaney was, but she doubted if moral scruples would keep him away from Stacey—after all, they hadn't kept him away from her.

'Anyway, don't go repeating what I've been saying,' Alice warned as they reached the end of the block.

'I don't gossip,' Kip returned coolly.

The older woman gave her a measuring look. 'No, you don't say much either, do you? Never met anyone with so little curiosity.'

'It's none of my business.' Kip resisted the other woman's interest in her and took her leave with a hurried, 'I have to go. I have to start work soon. Bye.'

She made up for any rudeness with a fleeting smile before taking to her heels.

She was genuinely in a hurry, but also she wanted to get away. In truth, she was curious about Whit Delaney—more so than she'd ever been about anyone else. But she had to fight it, had to forget. Forget how it had felt. In his arms. His body hard against hers. The breathless excitement. The final rush of pleasure just before the pain.

She shut her eyes but couldn't stop the camera in her head. Curiosity merged with jealousy as she thought of him doing the same thing with Stacey. Or was it just her? And why her? Had he shut *his* eyes and imagined her as someone else? His English wife, maybe?

Too many questions. Why had she agreed to lunch with his father? It was a crazy thing to do. She didn't need this

family. She needed no involvement. She had her running and
that was everything.

She resolved to cry off from the lunch. She tried the next
day, Friday. She telephoned first thing in the morning. She
expected to get Alice or Professor Delaney senior.

She wasn't ready for Whit Delaney saying, 'The Delaney
residence, Whitman speaking.'

'I...um...' Kip's throat was dry.

'Who is it, please?'

'No one... I mean, it doesn't—'

'Kipling,' he guessed from her mutterings, and added
quickly, 'Don't hang up... How are you?'

'I...' The enquiry threw Kip.

'My father says you're making great progress,' he continued at her silence.

'I...thanks.' She finally managed some response. 'I—it
was him I wanted to talk to.'

'Not in, I'm afraid,' he told her, 'but I can take a message.'

'Okay.' Kip cleared her throat in the hope of matching his
even tones. 'It's about Saturday...'

'You're coming to lunch, aren't you?' he picked up her
trailing sentence. 'My father's really looking forward to it.
He enjoys young company.'

Kip was reduced to silence once more. Was he doing it
purposely—making her feel guilty? Too guilty to cry off.

But why should he? She wasn't important to him one way
or the other. His tone told her that. He could manage to be
polite and friendly. She was the one stammering.

'I believe Mrs Novak is going to town too,' he added in
the same vein. 'She thinks you're in dire need of a good
square meal.'

He *was* doing it deliberately, Kip decided—making it
bloody impossible for her to back out.

'What time is lunch?' she finally asked. 'That's why I'm
phoning.'

He made some sound. Amused disbelief, perhaps. But he

was scrupulously pleasant as he replied, 'Usually twelve-thirty, but if that's a problem I'm sure they can switch it.'

'No problem,' she said. 'I'll be there.'

'Good,' he responded. 'It's just a pity I won't...I assume you know that.'

'Your father said something,' she admitted coolly.

This time he did give a brief laugh. 'Before you accepted the invitation, I imagine... Never mind; I'm glad you're coming, anyway.'

Kip frowned down the phone. Why should he be glad? Didn't he just want to forget? Maybe it wasn't an embarrassment to him.

'I'll see you some time, Kipling,' he added quietly.

A threat? A promise? A casual goodbye? Kip wasn't sure how to take it. She muttered a simple 'Bye,' before putting down the phone. She thought about it a while, then realised how foolish she was being.

She'd made him some kind of monster in her mind, but she had never rated beyond a mild indiscretion in his. He had probably slept with lots of girls. She was already history.

CHAPTER FIVE

'HELLO.' The bell was answered immediately by Abigail Delaney in a pretty floral dress.

Kip stared at her in surprise. She had assumed that the child would be absent as well.

'Hello,' she finally murmured to the small figure. 'I've come to lunch.'

'Yes, that's why I'm wearing a dress,' the girl declared forthrightly. 'Because a guest's coming.'

'Oh.' Kip detected no irony. 'Same here.'

Blue eyes—a reflection of her father's—watched as Kip took off her duffle-coat to reveal a red woollen polo neck and short kilt above black tights.

'That's not a dress,' said Abby, a very literal eight-year-old.

'It's the nearest I get.' Kip wasn't about to apologise for the fact.

Abby studied her dispassionately before announcing, 'It's cool.'

'Thanks,' Kip murmured drily.

They looked each other up and down for a moment longer before deciding on a mutual truce.

Alice Novak appeared at that moment. 'You're here, then. Lunch isn't quite ready yet.'

'She's coming upstairs to see my room,' Abby announced before Kip could respond.

'Mmm.' The housekeeper didn't look over-keen on the idea, but eventually muttered, 'All right. Make sure you come when I holler.'

'We will,' Abby agreed, and, grabbing hold of Kip's arm, half pulled her up the wooden staircase.

Kip went along with her because it was easier.

The girl's room was like the rest of the house—old-fashioned and quaint, with wooden flooring and faded rugs—but it had toys and pretty nick-nacks and a beautiful patchwork quilt on the bed that transformed it into a child's room.

Abby led her over to the seat at the big bay window which looked down on a long, haphazard garden that was carpeted with red autumn leaves.

'This was my daddy's room when he was little,' Abby said, and, before Kip could digest this, the child shoved a photograph frame into her hand. 'That's my mommy. Don't you think she's the most beautiful person you ever saw?'

Kip realised immediately that this was the purpose of her visit upstairs. She studied the woman in the photograph. The child wasn't exaggerating.

'She's very beautiful, yes.' Kip knew herself to be plain in comparison with the stunning blonde in the picture, who radiated sex apeal with a lazy smile.

Abby looked disappointed, as though she'd expected an argument. She tried again, stating mutinously, 'Stacey didn't think so. She said she looked too English, and I said that didn't make sense, because you're English and you don't look anything like my mother, and she said you were different—you don't look anything like anyone,' Abby relayed faithfully. 'I think she meant it to be nasty but I can't see how. It doesn't make sense either, does it?'

Kip shrugged. She wasn't going to use this child to trade insults with Stacey. 'I shouldn't worry about it.'

'No, well, *I* don't like *her* much,' Abby confided. 'She's all over me when my dad's around, then tells me to get lost when he isn't.'

'Perhaps you should tell him that,' Kip advised.

'I have—' Abby Delaney pulled a face '—but he doesn't believe me. He thinks I'm just trying to get rid of her...and I think he likes her, too.'

'Really?' Kip felt a dragging at the pit of her stomach.

'She's always making up to him.' Abby batted her eyes in imitation. 'It's gross…and he just doesn't see.' The girl shook her head over her father's short-sightedness.

'How old are you?' Kip wondered aloud.

'Eight,' Abby volunteered, 'but I seem older. That's because I'm very bright.'

Kip gave a short laugh at this solemn pronouncement. 'And modest too,' she countered drily, not expecting the girl to understand.

But Abby scowled in reply. 'I wasn't showing off, you know. I was just being honest. If you think it's fun being bright, you're wrong. The other kids pick on you, or expect you to do their homework for them, and even if you do they still don't talk to you.'

Kip had never had the problem of being considered over-bright, but she did remember being made to feel an oddity. 'It's the way kids are. They don't like kids who are different, so they dump on them.'

'Tell me about it!' Abby exclaimed in agreement, then gave Kip a measuring look. The verdict must have been favourable as she followed it with a smile. 'Have you ever considered going into the babysitting business?'

'Uh-uh—forget it.' Kip decided that quick disillusionment was required. 'I'm not suitable.'

The child was puzzled rather than put off by her answer. 'Why not? I think you're suitable.'

'Well, I'm not,' Kip denied, adding drily, 'For a start, I don't like children.'

Abby still wasn't discouraged. 'So? Stacey doesn't like children either. She just pretends. At least you wouldn't pretend.'

Kip had to admire her logic, but shook her head once more. 'Well, for another, I have a job,' she pointed out, and was rescued from making other excuses by the sound of Alice Novak's voice calling them to lunch.

'We'd better go,' she said as Abby's mouth turned down in a sulk.

'Don't want to,' the child said stubbornly.

'Suit yourself.' Kip wasn't prepared to argue or cajole. 'I'll tell them you don't want lunch.'

She walked off, out of the room and down the stairs.

'I didn't say that.' Abby clambered down after her, protesting angrily, and overtook her at the bottom.

Kip followed her through to the back of the house—not to the kitchen but to a small dining room with a table set for lunch.

Professor Delaney was already seated. He politely stood as she entered and welcomed her with a warm smile. 'I hear Abby's been entertaining you.'

Abby looked daggers at her, expecting her to betray her latest rudeness, but Kip wouldn't have dreamt of it.

She said simply, 'She showed me her room,' and went to sit where he indicated.

'I showed her my mommy's picture,' Abby announced in a slightly challenging tone.

It did not have the desired effect, as the old professor smiled easily, saying, 'That's nice, honey,' then directed at Kip, 'Perhaps you've heard—Abby's mother died last year and naturally Abby misses her.'

'No, I don't,' was muttered under the child's breath.

Seated opposite her, Kip still caught the words. If the Professor did—Kip knew that he was slightly deaf in his left ear—he decided to ignore it.

'That looks absolutely delicious, Alice.' He smiled as the housekeeper appeared with the first course. 'Why don't you sit down and share it with us?'

The invitation was greeted with one of Alice's snorts, but she looked pleased none the less before declaring, 'I'll be having mine in the kitchen, if it's all the same with you.'

It wasn't a question but a statement given as she retreated, and he explained, 'Alice eats with us when we eat in the kitchen, but she won't join us if we have a guest. Doesn't think it's fitting,' he confided with a fond smile.

Abby had no such fondness for the housekeeper. 'That's because she's a servant.'

'Abby.' Her grandfather gave her a disappointed look.

The girl had the grace to blush, even as she said in her own defence, 'That's what she calls herself.'

'I know,' her grandfather granted her, 'but that's not how I look on her. She's been a good friend to this family and deserves our respect.'

The child's blush deepened. Her grandfather's gentle disapproval quelled her in a way that shouts and threats never would.

'I'm afraid Abby and Alice don't always see eye to eye,' the professor told Kip. 'It's hard for Alice. She brought up children in an era when they were seen, not heard, and doesn't believe in too much freedom of expression. Abby, on the other hand, has had a very liberal upbringing.'

Whether Abby understood the word 'liberal' or not, Kip wasn't sure, but she certainly caught the gist, claiming to Kip, 'I used to get to do exactly what I wanted all the time.'

Some reply was obviously expected from her, so Kip answered honestly, 'I imagine that can be quite difficult.'

'Difficult?' Abby was clearly surprised by the comment. 'Why?'

'Well, when you're young, some things are dangerous or bad for you. Like crossing busy roads or eating too many sweets or staying up late.' Kip's tone was factual rather than patronising, so Abby listened rather than sulked. 'Most kids don't have to worry about it, though, because their parents decide for them. But if you have to decide for yourself it must be harder.'

Kip wasn't quite sure if she was making sense, but Abby obviously thought that she was. 'It is…much!' the girl agreed with feeling. 'Like the movies on TV. I used to watch ones late at night—scary ones—and I kinda liked them and kinda didn't. Then I'd have bad dreams, so I knew I shouldn't watch, but it was hard not to. The same with eating too much ice cream, then feeling sick. It's easier if your mom stops you.'

Alex Delaney nodded attentively. 'Do you know, I've never really considered things from that viewpoint? But you're right. After all, it's hard enough as an adult to assume responsibility for your actions… But, in that case,' he turned to ask Abby, 'why do you mind so much when Alice tells you not to do something?'

'It's the way she tells me,' Abby declared after a moment's thought. 'She thinks I'm too stupid to work out things for myself and that's just as bad as being expected to work out everything. That Stacey creature's the same.'

'Abby!' her grandfather reproved her.

'It's what Alice calls her,' Abby said in her defence. 'I've heard her.'

'That's different,' Alex Delaney responded, and explained to Kip, 'Stacey is one of Abby's babysitters… Weren't you in the same literature class?'

Kip nodded.

It was Abby who chipped in, 'But they didn't like each other. Not surprised either. Who'd like Stacey?'

He frowned at his granddaughter, before saying to Kip, 'I assume Abby is exaggerating—or is there a problem with Stacey?'

Kip felt on the spot. Personally she wouldn't let Stacey look after her dog if she had one. But who was she to claim the other girl as not good enough to mind children?

'Stacey and I aren't friends,' she answered truthfully, 'but that might be me as much as her.'

It was a wishy-washy reply that avoided specifics. Abby, who had been willing her to suggest that Stacey might have homicidal tendencies, gave her a baleful look.

The old professor wasn't altogether satisfied either, but he decided to drop the subject for now. Instead he asked her, 'As a point of interest, whose choice was Kipling? Your mother's or your father's?'

'Both, I think.' Kip didn't mind this Delaney's curiosity. 'My father wanted to call me Kip after a famous Kenyan runner.'

'Kipchoge Keino.' The old professor surprised her with his knowledge.

'Yes, that's the one.' Kip nodded. 'My father was a great admirer. My mother wasn't so keen, though she was an athlete too. She changed it to Kipling, just in case I turned out to be more literary than athletic... Bit of an irony, in retrospect.' Kip gave a brief laugh.

'I wouldn't be too sure.' The professor realised what she meant. 'You may have problems with the technicalities of reading, Kipling, but I feel—and so does my son—that your comprehension is far beyond the majority of our students.'

Kip smiled a little, warmed by the compliment, although she wished that he hadn't included his son's opinion. It reminded her that she was currently sitting with Whit Delaney's daughter and father, and had no business to be doing so. Not if she had any sense.

'What problems?' Abby asked of no one in particular, and, lacking a response, ran on, 'I had a problem once. I couldn't tell my Bs from my Ds, but I could still read.'

'Abby!' The professor looked repressively at his granddaughter, then grimaced in apology at Kip.

She shrugged, taking no offence. She was getting used to the child's precociousness. She was even beginning to like her a little.

Abby seemed to return the feeling. Perhaps because she couldn't shock Kip or upset her she had decided that she might as well like her.

The rest of the meal passed pleasantly enough, and they lingered over coffee until Alice appeared to say, 'That Stacey creature's come to take her ladyship to the Pearsons.'

Abby protested immediately, 'Aw, no! Can't I stay with you two?'

''Fraid not,' her grandfather said with a kindly smile. 'Kipling and I have work to do.'

'I could work too,' Abby suggested. 'I could sit and do sums or a story, or read a book or something.'

Her grandfather's brows rose. 'Stacey must be bad,' he said at her offer, and confided to Kip, 'Normally Whit has to twist Abby's arm to do any studying.

'So, can I?' Abby pleaded.

'No, you can't,' came from Alice Novak, perhaps because she saw her employer begin to weaken. 'Your dad's arranged for you to go play with Dr Pearson's daughter, so you run along and get your coat on and Stacey will take you there.'

'Aw!' Abby protested once more, but, receiving no support from her grandfather, marched noisily out of the room.

'She's a handful, I must admit,' he sighed. 'But it wasn't easy for her when my son and daughter-in-law parted... Still, you can't want to hear all this,' he added, with an apologetic smile.

He was wrong. Kip found herself wondering what had happened in Whit Delaney's marriage. Had he chased after women, girls? Was that why his actress wife had left?

Kip imagined that that must be unbearable—to love someone utterly, then discover he'd been unfaithful. She was glad that she would never love like that. It wasn't in her nature.

'Well, we'd better get to work.' Professor Delaney rose from his chair as Alice bustled in to tidy up the table.

Kip followed him through to his study and they worked for three hours, with a brief break for another coffee.

'The progress you've made in just a few weeks is quite phenomenal,' the professor declared at the end of the afternoon, when he read the piece of work she'd done for him. 'In fact, I can't understand why you ever had a problem. The tests indicate that you aren't dyslexic, even in a mild form... Have you ever had hearing difficulties?'

'I'm not sure.' Kip cast her mind back to childhood. 'I remember when I was little thinking that all teachers seemed to speak very quietly... But I can hear fine now.'

'Perhaps you had some hearing loss as a younger child,' the professor speculated. 'That certainly would have retarded your reading progress... I'm just surprised no one ever picked up on it or helped you later.'

'There was one teacher—Miss Wilkie,' Kip related. 'She gave me some help after school for a while, but then we moved again.'

'Weren't your parents worried?' Alex Delaney frowned.

'There was just my father. My mother died when I was very little,' she replied, 'and—well...my father had his own problems.'

Like trying to hold down a job and drink at the same time, Kip recalled, but didn't share the fact. She already regretted telling Whit Delaney about her father.

'*Had?*' The older Delaney picked up her use of the past tense.

'My father's dead too now,' she said tonelessly.

'I'm sorry,' the professor said with genuine sympathy. 'Do you have any brothers or sisters?'

She shook her head. 'No, there's just me.'

'So, who will you be going home to,' he ran on, 'at Christmas?'

Kip could have told the truth—that she had no one to return to—but the old professor was already looking at her with gentle pity in his eye.

'I have an aunt in Leeds,' she confided. It was perfectly true. Her father's sister, Pat. She had come to his funeral because it had been the right thing to do, but had shown little warmth for Kip. In fact, her strongest feeling had appeared to be satisfaction. She had predicted that her younger brother would come to a bad end and she had been proved right. Her grudging offer to give Kip a home had been promptly turned down.

Professor Delaney nodded with satisfaction, thinking that Kip meant to spend the festive season with this aunt, and dropped the subject.

'I have to go,' Kip said, glancing at her watch.

'Ah, Saturday night.' The Professor's eyes twinkled as he concluded, 'Doubtless, a lovely girl such as yourself has a date.'

Colour filled Kip's cheeks. She knew that the professor was being kind. She didn't see herself as 'lovely' so she was sure that no one else did.

Professor Delaney took her blush as confirmation, although, in fact, the only place she had to go was to work at Sam's pizza parlour. 'I'll have to tell my son.'

'Why?' Kip countered a little sharply.

Professor Delaney looked taken aback. 'No special reason,' he said, shaking his head. 'It's just that he imagines you have no social life outside the track. So what's his name? Or shouldn't I ask?'

'I…Tom.' She said the first name that came into her head.

'Tom,' the professor repeated. 'A student, I presume?'

She nodded. 'He's on the athletics team,' she said before she had time to think, then almost instantly regretted it. She didn't need to embroider the lie. She hadn't needed to lie in the first place. Why had she?

'Well, bring him round some time if you like,' the professor suggested as he showed Kip to the door.

'I…thanks,' Kip said at this surprise invitation, and wondered if the guilt she felt was written in block capitals on her face.

Seemingly not, as Professor Delaney smiled benignly, then gave her a wave from the top step.

Kip waved back and called a belated, 'Thanks for lunch,' before hurrying up the avenue. It had been a good afternoon and she'd had to go and spoil it by telling some silly lie.

Not that she hadn't lied before. Her later school years had included numerous absences covered by inventive excuses. But she hated lying to people she liked, and she liked the old professor.

Why had she lied? She asked herself the same question four days later when Whit Delaney appeared without warning as she completed a lunchtime workout in the college gym. With three or so weeks to Christmas, Kip was one of the few athletes still in serious training.

'Coach suggested I'd find you here,' he explained as he came to sit beside her on a bench.

'So?' Kip dropped her eyes from his and picked up a towel to wipe the sweat from her face.

'He also said if I did find you here,' Whit continued, 'to ask you what the hell you're doing. He told you to take a break, I understand.'

'I am taking a break.' Kip had cut down on her mileage per day. 'I was just doing some light training.'

'Didn't look particularly light from where I was standing,' Whit countered drily.

Kip glanced at him, wondering how long he'd been watching her, then glanced away from the sharp blue eyes still watching her.

'What do you want?' she switched to asking.

'Nothing specific,' he responded. 'I just thought I'd see how you were getting on.'

His tone reflected genuine concern and Kip's heart lifted. Maybe he hadn't forgotten. Maybe he thought of her, as she did of him, unable to stop herself.

Then his voice hardening, he asked, 'Who's Tom?'

'Tom?' She stared at him blankly.

Whit jogged her memory. 'My father says he's on the athletics team.'

He watched her go red. What did that mean? She was now sleeping with this boy too?

'He's no one you know,' she finally retorted, with a scowl that said, Mind your own business.

Whit wished that he could, but the girl—or what he had done to her—kept nagging at his conscience.

'How serious is it?' He tried to sound neutral when he actually wanted to ask if they were making out—teenage language but she wasn't much older than that.

'Well, we're not sending out wedding invitations yet,' she responded, tongue-in-cheek.

He laughed drily, though he half felt like shaking her. She was a funny kid. It was as if she were twelve and forty at the same time. Streetwise yet breakable, too.

'Well, I'm glad you're dating, anyway,' he said in a more paternal vein.

This time she looked at him as if he were mad, and Whit wondered if he might be. He was certainly lying. He wasn't glad that she was dating. He couldn't get his head round it at all.

He caught and held her eyes for a moment, and they dragged him back to that one time. Him and her, on her bed. He couldn't quite remember how they'd landed there, but he remembered all too well the rest. Her body, soft and slick with sweat, surprisingly full breasts, a dark triangle of hair. He closed his eyes and shut off the picture before it became a full-scale fantasy once more.

He said what he had come to say—or blurted it out was perhaps closer to the mark. 'Are you pregnant?'

'What?' She stared at him in shock for a moment.

'Are you pregnant?' He repeated the question and saw from her expression that she hadn't even considered the possibility. 'It's not likely, I know. We didn't have full sexual intercourse as such, but I did enter you.'

He hadn't meant to speak so clinically. It had just come out that way. She didn't make it any easier—staring at him with those large green eyes that betrayed no emotion.

'I'm not pregnant,' she eventually replied, clear-cut and clinical as he had been.

It should have been a relief. No indignation. No hysterics. Just a straight answer. But her very calmness made him distrustful.

'Are you sure?' He needed to hear it again.

'I'm sure,' she said, and, assuming that that was the end of the conversation, stood to go.

He stood with her and grabbed her wrist when she would have walked away. 'Because if you were we'd work things out together,' he added, meaning what he said.

But it was hardly surprising that she looked at him with total derision. 'Really? You give me the money and I go to a clinic? Is that how we'd work it out *together*, Professor?'

The reason he sometimes liked this girl was exactly the same reason why he disliked her now. There was no pretence about her. No phoniness. No concession to the conventions that helped keep the rest of the world in some kind of order. She went for the jugular and didn't care how much blood was spilled.

He felt his own leaking out of him, and said, 'What do you want of me? I'm trying to do the right thing.'

'Then stay away.' Kip slipped from his grip and said, before her voice could break. 'Stay away from me.'

She half walked, half ran into the changing room, and sat there, shaking with reaction.

Was she pregnant? She had no idea. She hadn't even considered it. She thought because they had stopped…but, of course, he might be right. She didn't know that much about these things, and, like many women athletes, her body cycle was far from regular. She could be pregnant.

She shook her head. No, it was an absurd idea. She couldn't be. She couldn't have a baby. She didn't know how to look after one—or love it.

Rage had held Kip together when he'd suggested the idea, but now panic threatened to blow her apart. She collected her things and didn't even wait to shower. She walked to a pharmacist's in a shopping mall, well away from the college, and bought a kit—one that promised instant results. Then she went to a Ladies' powder room in a department store, followed the instructions and waited in the end cubicle, oblivious of the stream of women going in and out.

It was the worst few minutes of her life. She told herself that the chances of a dark ring appearing were almost negligible. She told herself that God wouldn't give a baby to someone who couldn't care for it. She also told herself that there were thousands of kids running around who disproved the theory.

No dark ring appeared. She should have felt relieved. Instead she felt dazed and empty.

She walked on automatic, out of the store and the shopping mall. She was still on automatic when she reached the street. She didn't look. She stepped off the pavement and didn't look. Slow as it was travelling, the car had no chance of avoiding her.

It hit her side-on—a glancing blow that threw her back on the pavement. She struck her head but remained conscious for a moment or two. Conscious of the surprise of it, then the people, then the searing pain in her leg. Her leg. It brought her back to reality and made her forget babies that had never been.

My leg! she screamed inside, but it came out a whisper as she finally passed out.

CHAPTER SIX

KIP regained consciousness in the emergency room of the county hospital. Her tracksuit top was eased off her by a nurse; another had already cut away her trousers to reveal the damage. The pain was relentless.

She gritted her teeth and managed to say, 'My leg?' But neither seemed to hear her and she slipped away again.

She didn't know whether she was gone seconds or hours. The next time she opened her eyes it was to find two doctors examining her injuries. She could see that they were touching her foot but she couldn't feel it.

She tried to speak to them; the words were a slurred mess in her head. But she could hear their conversation, though it seemed at a distance.

'There's been no blood to it for nearly two hours,' the older doctor stated in final tones. 'It's just not viable.'

'We could try microsurgery to the artery,' his younger colleague volunteered. 'What's there to lose?'

'Your time and the hospital's money,' the more senior man retorted. 'Face facts. The foot is lost. I suggest you call Theatre and just get on with it, Dr Shutkever.'

'Yes, Dr Paul,' his junior said on a defeated note.

The medical terms meant nothing to Kip. She understood just one phrase. 'The foot is lost.' She watched in horror as the older doctor walked away, his verdict delivered.

Kip would be the one to serve the sentence—a life sentence if she lost her foot.

She wanted to cry out, but all she could manage was a whimper. 'Dr...'

It was enough to bring the younger doctor to her side.

'You've been in an accident, but you're going to be all right. We'll take you down to the operating theatre and fix your leg.'

'No.' Kip shook her head and made a supreme effort to say, 'My foot; you can't...not my foot.'

The doctor dropped his reassuring air as he realised that she had overheard. He took refuge in medical terms. Though it was a minor accident, she had fractured the ends of her tibia and fibula and her foot had been twisted at an awkward angle. Pressure on the artery had led to a lack of circulation to the foot and total loss of function.

Kip heard little. She just repeated, 'You can't...' And her eyes held his in mute appeal.

It seemed to move him, then he called over, 'Nurse, this patient requires ten milligrams of morphine.'

Kip felt herself slipping away. She tried to sit up. It sent a blinding pain through her head but kept her conscious.

'Please...' she tried one last time.

'I'm sorry,' the doctor said as silent tears slipped down her face, 'but there's nothing we can do... Give her another shot, Nurse.'

The nurse did as she was told. She pushed up the sleeve of Kip's gown. Kip was too weak to resist. The drug took hold and smothered her in darkness.

Over the next few hours she drifted in and out of consciousness but made little sense of what was happening to her.

At one stage she seemed to be back in the ambulance, travelling to hospital. At another she could see the doctors leaning over, once more in discussion, but now their faces had changed. She remembered ceilings and lights as she was wheeled to Theatre. She remembered tearing pain when she came round from the operation, but she was quickly returned to dreamland.

It was the early hours of the morning before she became fully conscious. She woke to find herself in a hospital bed. She was curtained off from whoever else was occupying the ward. She gasped in pain as she moved slightly. Her leg still hurt, especially her foot.

Only it couldn't. Because she no longer had one. Kip didn't remember everything, but she remembered that. She had lost her foot. No, they had taken it away, and left in its place a lump of plaster. She could feel it with her other leg. She lay there, uncomplaining of the pain in her leg, for it was nothing compared to the devastation in her soul. Her life was over.

Somehow she slept, and when she woke next winter sunlight filtered in through her curtains. A nurse arrived, bustling with efficiency and goodwill, but Kip made no response. The nurse drew the curtains and tried to introduce the woman in the second bed in the room. Kip didn't hear her, or didn't want to. She turned away and bore her misery in silence.

It was strange, seeing her lying still in her hospital bed. Whit was used to her on the move, rushing everywhere, running from him.

The woman in the other bed stared in curiosity as he crossed the room. Kip didn't seem to notice him. Her head was turned to the wall. He acknowledged the other woman with a brief nod of politeness, before drawing the curtain between the two beds.

Kip remained inert. For a moment he wondered if she was asleep, but her eyes were open, staring into space.

'Kip.' He spoke her name quietly.

She still started in surprise. A myriad of emotions crossed her face before she settled on that closed-in, resentful look. She certainly wasn't pleased to see him.

'What are you doing here?' she finally asked.

'The hospital said you'd regained consciousness,' he explained briefly, 'so I drove up... How are you feeling?'

'Fine!' she spat the word at him, closely following it with, 'I'm not pregnant so you can stop worrying.'

'What?' Whit felt that he'd missed part of the conversation.

'I did a test,' she ran on, 'and there was no ring. It was in my bag but I don't know where it is.'

Whit was still trying to catch up. The last they'd talked of this had been in the college gymnasium, and she'd been emphatic then. Had she lied? Had he put the idea in her head, and, uncertain, she'd gone and bought a home test?

'When did you do this test?' He received no reply and concluded for himself. 'Just before the accident? Was that it?'

'Does it matter?' she threw back, with visible contempt for him. 'There's no baby so you don't have to come here pretending concern.'

'I'm not pretending,' he replied heavily, 'and I'm not here because of some baby you already told me didn't exist. Remember?'

'Then why?' Her green eyes narrowed in distrust.

'God knows!' Whit said in exasperation, and asked himself the same question.

He'd known that she wouldn't want his help, but yesterday she'd been in no state to refuse it. It had been his father who had involved him. A young doctor had called Alex Delaney at home. Apparently theirs was the only address she had in her bag. His father had relayed the situation to Whit and he had reacted accordingly. He'd done all that could be done for her. He didn't expect any thanks for it.

'I don't need your pity.' Her eyes were fierce with pride.

'Too right, you don't,' he agreed, losing patience. 'You're already feeling more than enough for yourself. You've hurt your leg. It's hardly the end of the world. There's even a slim chance you'll run again.' He switched from sympathy to the plain talking she seemed to prefer.

She looked shocked for a moment. Obviously she could dish it out but not take it. Her eyes filled with something suspiciously like tears before she turned her head back to the wall.

Whit had known women who used tears as a weapon. She wasn't one of them. He felt that curious mixture of anger and guilt that she always made him feel.

He moved round to the other side of the bed and caught her face in his hand before she could turn away from him again. A tear was rolling down her cheek. He wiped it away with his finger, but it was closely followed by another. She shut her eyes against the betraying tears—against him.

'Look, Kip, I do understand—' He spoke softly again, but she didn't give him a chance to finish.

'You don't!' Her voice was bitter and unsteady at one and the same time. 'I've lost my foot. Tell me how I'm going to run, Professor!'

This time Whit was caught by surprise. She was right. He didn't understand.

'Kip, listen to me,' he urged quietly. 'Have you seen a doctor yet?'

Kip shook her head, then looked in bewilderment as he carefully lifted the sheets and blankets off the end of her bed. A metal cage protected her plastered leg. She could see little from the angle at which she lay.

'Can you feel this?' he asked.

'No...yes,' Kip changed what she was saying as she felt a small tickling sensation somewhere beneath the general pain that was her leg.

'That was your big toe,' Whit told her drily, 'which very much looks as though it's still attached to your foot, which presumably is still attached to your leg, somewhere beneath that plaster.'

Kip looked at him in disbelief. 'It can't be. I heard a doctor say they were going to take my foot off.'

'Initially it was thought they'd have to,' Whit confirmed, 'but one of the young doctors felt there might be a chance if they could draft in a trauma specialist to do microsurgery. That's why you were transferred here.'

Kip stared down at her leg and asked absently, 'Where is here?'

'Boston Heights.'

'In Boston?'

He smiled at the question. 'Naturally.'

Kip realised that she hadn't imagined it, the second ambulance ride. She had been speeding the thirty miles to the city.

It was like being given a second chance in life. Kip was literally able to smile through the pain.

Whit could have left things that way, only it seemed wrong to raise her hopes too high.

'I spoke to the specialist this morning. He believes the operation was a success, but,' he continued, on a note of caution, 'he can't promise a return to absolute fitness.'

She caught on quickly. 'I may not run competitively again?'

He nodded, trying to read her reaction. It was hard. He'd expected despair, and perhaps that was what was going on behind the shuttered expression she wore.

'It's over, then.' She spoke to herself.

But Whit guessed that 'it' was her reason for being—the dream, the glory, the thing that kept her from recognising the crashing emptiness of her life. Whit wanted to rage against whoever or whatever had made this girl so terrifyingly single-minded. But now wasn't the time to say that there were more things in life than running round a racetrack, chasing medals that might always be out of reach.

'That said, the specialist didn't rule it out.' Whit gave her something to hold onto, slim hope though it might be. 'The cast will be removed in about seven weeks. After that you'll have intensive physiotherapy. With the right recovery programme, who knows what the prognosis is?'

She showed little enthusiasm. 'Won't that cost money? I have no medical insurance.'

Whit knew that well enough. Her lack of insurance had almost cost her her foot. If that young doctor hadn't bothered contacting them, she would have got no further than the basic care at Radford County.

'That won't be a problem. The college has cover for its injured athletes.' He made it up off the top of his head, but it sounded convincing enough.

She saw a flaw. 'That'll be ones injured on the track, won't it?'

'No, it's regardless,' he claimed, lying outright. 'I've checked with Bill Scott, your coach.'

'Oh.' Her face lit up as he revived the dream for her.

Her running really was everything to her, Whit realised. Those green eyes had never looked so intently at him. He just prayed that if her injuries did prove to be permanently debilitating she could find some other aim in life at which to direct all that burning energy.

'For the moment,' he continued, 'you're just going to have to learn to take things easy. It'll be some time before you're out of here, and then it'll be on crutches.'

Kip's face fell once more. 'Sam. Has anyone told Sam what's happened?'

'Sam?'

'My boss at the pizza parlour. He'll be wondering why I haven't turned up for work.' Kip bit her lip as she began to realise the other consequences of her accident. No job. No apartment. No money. The college might pay her hospital bills, but it wouldn't take care of her living expenses.

'Don't worry about that; I'll talk to him,' he dismissed. 'Just concentrate on getting better.'

'Yes.' Kip decided that he was right. The loss of her job was nothing compared to the loss she might have sustained.

'You're looking tired,' Whit added. 'I'll go now and come back tomorrow.'

'No, it's OK,' Kip assured him. 'You've done enough already.'

Whit wasn't fooled. 'And you'd sooner have Genghis Khan as a visitor?'

Kip didn't deny it. Her blush revealed all. 'I suppose I should be grateful,' she made herself say.

'Not especially.' Whatever Whit wanted from this girl, it wasn't gratitude. 'Is there someone I should contact? My father says you have an aunt in Leeds.'

Kip shook her head. 'No, not her.'

'All right.' Whit accepted her right of choice. 'My father would like to visit. Is that OK?'

This time Kip nodded. Alex Delaney was no threat. It was only Whit who disturbed her.

He rose to go, and on some impulse took her hand in his. He squeezed her fingers briefly. It was a goodbye.

Kip felt shaken, warm then cold as he walked away. He would not come again.

But his father came. Despite the distance, Alex Delaney travelled up almost every day. Kip worried about his health but he dismissed her fears, saying that the train journey was no hardship. He brought her books to read and study, and they continued her tuition in hospital.

It was a revelation: to read with a fluency that allowed her to appreciate the language and ideas of a book rather than just the basic meaning. It was like being blind and suddenly seeing, and, with the fervour of a recent convert, she devoured the books that the professor gave her—novels, poetry, biographies, texts on grammar and correct English.

'Whit is going to be confounded!' the professor declared when he read the critique that she'd done on a novel.

Kip frowned at this mention of Whit Delaney. She hadn't seen him since his first and last visit ten days earlier. She had told him not to come so it was quite ridiculous that she felt abandoned. Yet she did.

'I understand you've been given your release date,' Alex Delaney went on.

Kip nodded. 'Friday.'

'What are you going to do?' he added.

'I haven't decided yet,' Kip said, as if she had some choice, when the truth was that she probably had none.

'Well, Whit's going to come and talk to you,' the old professor said, 'but I can't see any harm in my asking you... We'd like you to come and stay with us while you recover.'

'At your house?' Kip wanted to be sure that she understood.

He nodded. 'There's lots of room, and we're all happy about it.'

'Including Whi—Professor Delaney?' Kip couldn't believe that Whitman would want her there.

Yet his father claimed otherwise. 'It was his idea. And Abby's delighted too. Mrs Novak's already made up a room for you downstairs. It's at the back of the house, overlooking the garden, so it should afford you some privacy... Whit felt that would be important to you.'

Kip remained in a state of disbelief. In fact, she might have told the professor that he had it wrong if she hadn't been used to the inconsistencies in his son's behaviour. Instead she kept quiet while he outlined their plans for her, and lay puzzling over Whit Delaney's motives when he was gone.

She didn't have to puzzle long. The man himself appeared later that afternoon. She'd been napping and woke to find him at the foot of her bed.

He smiled as she woke, and waited until she sat up a little before he presented her with the flowers in his hand.

Still drowsy, Kip struggled with a mixture of emotions: confusion, then a curious pain in her chest, followed quickly by anger.

She didn't express any of these feelings as he stood looking down at her. Instead she glanced towards the other bed in the room. Its normal occupant, Maggie, was sitting in a wheelchair on the far side.

The woman had been watching televison but she was now watching them. As well as a broken hip, Maggie Carson suffered from terminal curiosity.

'May I use this chair?' Whit directed at the other woman.

'Sure, help yourself.' Maggie returned his smile with a hundred-watt one of her own and a fluttering of false eyelashes.

Kip's lips compressed, disgusted with both. Knowing that Maggie would listen to every word, she was relieved when a nurse appeared to wheel the other woman away for a shower.

'See you soon,' Maggie called out, ostensibly to Kip, but Whit was her real target.

He seemed oblivious. He sat down and scrutinised Kip once more. 'You look better. You've put on some weight.'

'Thanks... Have you ever considered the diplomatic service?' she threw back.

'That wasn't meant as an insult,' he assured her. 'You were too skinny before.'

Kip continued to look resentful. What gave him the right to comment on her appearance?

'I have something to tell you.' His manner became more sympathetic. 'It's about your apartment. Your boss says he's sorry but—'

'He's kicking me out,' Kip concluded for him.

He nodded. 'More or less. He'll let you have it until the New Year, but I gather he's promised it to his new waitress after that.'

None of this came as a surprise to Kip. Sam had always been fair to her, but never sentimental. Letting her stay on through Christmas was stretching the limits of his charity.

'What are you going to do?' Whit added when she made no comment.

Kip wondered what answer he expected. Was she meant to throw herself on his mercy? Or was the offer to put her up really his father's idea and he was waiting for a let-out? That must be it.

'I've decided to go home,' she said, as though it was all cut and dried.

'Home?' he echoed. 'To England, you mean?'

'Yes, I have an aunt in Leeds.' She used her father's sister again, although she'd sooner have spent Christmas in a Salvation Army hostel. It might come down to that.

'The same aunt in Leeds that you didn't want contacted,' he drawled back, 'even after you'd been knocked down by a car.'

Kip glared in return. What did he want from her? An admission that she had no real family?

'I didn't want to worry her,' she replied heavily.

'I can buy that.' He nodded. 'Just give me her number and I'll phone now. Tell her you'll be home for Christmas... After all, she's going to have to collect you from the airport.'

'I can manage,' she claimed.

'In a wheelchair? Or on crutches? And with a suitcase?' He pointed out some slight obstacles.

'I'll take a taxi.' Why was he being so damn difficult?

'A taxi,' he echoed. 'From Heathrow to Leeds? How far is that again? Two hundred miles? Three hundred? That's one great fare for some London cabby... By the way, Sam says not to worry about the rent; he'll just take it out of your last wage.'

Kip's glare turned to a look of intense dislike. He knew it all. He knew that she had no job, no place to stay, no money even for an air ticket.

'Well, don't worry. I won't be going home with you!' she declared angrily.

'Who's inviting you?' he flipped back.

'Your father.' It brought a surprised look to his face. 'He was here earlier.'

'Damn,' he muttered under his breath, but she caught it all the same.

'I said, Don't worry,' she repeated. 'I'd sooner bed down at the YWCA than take up residence in your house.'

'Now who's being insulting?' he countered. 'But, just for the record, it's my father's house, not mine, and the local Y is a five-storey with no lifts.'

He looked pointedly at her leg. It was plastered to the knee.

He became even blunter as he went on, 'I guess you've given up, then. Thrown in the tracksuit? Hung up your spikes? Run your last race?'

'I didn't say that,' Kip denied angrily.

'Didn't you?' He arched an eyebrow. 'I just assumed you were calling it a day. I mean, if you leave college now you'll have lost your scholarship and the coaching facilities that went along with it. Still, if you think you can't come back from the injury—'

'I didn't say that,' Kip cut in furiously. 'I didn't say anything like that.'

'Not in so many words—' he shrugged '—but if you're not going to stay with my father, how else are you going to remain in Radford and keep up your studies?'

Kip had no answer, because there wasn't one. The Delaneys were her only chance, but she hated him for saying so.

'You can't want me staying there,' she muttered back.

'All the more reason for you to do so, I would have thought.' He acknowledged her animosity, and, without giving her a chance to argue further, got to his feet and announced, 'I'll collect you Friday.'

Kip watched him go, with mixed feelings. She knew that she should be thanking him but all she felt was resentment. It was the first time in years that she'd had to rely on someone else, and the someone else being Whit Delaney only made it worse.

She wasn't given time to brood over the matter as her room companion reappeared from her shower. A woman in her early forties, Maggie had showed an offhand curiosity about Kip on her arrival, and, getting scant information out of her, had then volunteered her own life story of past successes as a singer, followed by broken love affairs and personal tragedies.

'Who was Kris Kristofferson's double, girl?' Maggie's eyes narrowed in interest.

Kip looked blank. 'Kris Kristofferson?'

'Country and Western singer?' Maggie prompted, and, when it elicited no response, started singing a song that Kip didn't recognise either.

Maggie shook her head over Kip's ignorance and added, 'So who was he?'

'My professor,' Kip replied cagily.

'Your professor? Oh, yeah,' Maggie laughed throatily, thinking it a joke. 'I thought the old guy was your professor.'

'They both are,' Kip claimed.

Unconvinced, Maggie drawled back, 'Well, if I'd known professors could be like that, I'd have gone to college myself.'

'Like what?' Kip challenged rashly.

'Like he could give you the best weekend of your life!' Maggie declared with crude emphasis, and only laughed more loudly as Kip's cheeks went a deep red. 'The way he was looking at you, I guess you've already had the weekend.'

'Don't be stupid!' Kip felt indignant even if she wasn't quite entitled to be. 'Is that all you think about?'

Maggie lifted a surprised brow. Up till then, Kip had been a fairly passive room mate.

'Pretty much, yes,' she admitted with a wicked smile. 'But, don't worry, girl, your secret's safe with me.'

'My secret?' Kip frowned darkly.

'Well, maybe I've got it wrong,' Maggie said, wheeling herself back to the open door, 'but from where I was sitting your professor didn't seem the only one with the love light in his eyes.'

The words 'that's ridiculous' rose to Kip's lips, but she didn't get a chance to say them as Maggie made a rapid getaway.

So she said the words to herself. I don't love him. I can't love him. I mustn't love him. She said the words like a counterspell to the confusion of feeling inside her. She said the words even as she admitted the truth to herself. She wanted Whit Delaney. She wanted him in the worst way.

But that was just sex. Chemistry. Biology. Whatever damn science governed these things. Not love. Never love. Even Kip knew the difference, though she'd loved no one in her life but her father—and that had been difficult enough to sustain.

She thought of her father now rather than think of Whit Delaney. It was scarcely more comforting. The last time she'd seen him had been in a hospital too. His liver had been shot and he'd had the complexion of a drinker. It had been pitiful. She'd kept looking at him and recalling a photograph they'd had at home. In it he'd been twenty-four and at the high point of his athletics career, a silver medallist at the Commonwealth Games. He had been fit and tanned and on top of the world, believing an Olympic gold was just round the next corner.

Instead there had been injury—a torn ligament that was to mend, then tear again, and finally put paid to his dreams.

He hadn't fallen apart immediately. He'd met Kip's mother, at nineteen already rated as a distance runner. He'd taken over her coaching, helped her to a bronze at the World Championships and married her along the way. With a year out for a baby, they'd set their sights on the Olympics. Nothing could stop them—nothing but the cruel, senseless cancer that had raced through her body and killed their dreams.

Kip had kept thinking of that photograph as she'd sat with her father and she'd felt like weeping. Not for the man dying by inches before her, but for the man who had died long ago. He hadn't wanted her tears, though. He'd wanted her promise that she would keep running and win the medals that he and her mother had been cheated out of. And she had given it— that promise.

Two years on she still felt bound by it.

So she had no real choice. With her leg in plaster, and crutches her only way to get about, she couldn't work. Without work, she was broke and homeless. If she wanted to remain in America and fight back to fitness, she needed the Delaneys.

But it was hard. She knew that she should be grateful. She tried to feel it or at least show it, when Whit came to collect her on Friday. She talked to him in monosyllables, but they were scrupulously polite monosyllables. Each time he helped her she thanked him, but it was a strain because she hated her need for help.

He must have known it. As they drew to a halt on Washington Avenue he turned and said, 'Look, can we cut out the forced thank-yous? I'm not doing this for gratitude.'

'Then why?' Kip dropped the pretence.

He followed suit, saying, 'Guilt, I suppose. I took something from you I shouldn't. I can't give it back, so I guess this is penance instead.'

It was a moment before Kip realised what he meant, what he had taken. Her virginity. Kip's cheeks filled with colour. From memory she knew that she hadn't tried to hold onto it very hard. Possibly he valued it more highly than she herself had.

She had heard only sincerity in Whit's voice and she promised in return, 'I'll never tell anyone.'

He shook his head. 'That's not what this is about. I'm not trying to silence you.'

'I know.' Kip understood that. As a best-selling writer, Whit was above small-town scandal. It was his own conscience that he was answering, as was Kip in saying, 'You don't have to do any of this. You owe me nothing. I was…I was willing,' she admitted in a rush of honesty and embarrassment.

'Were you?' He looked straight at her and she looked back for a moment, and something in his eyes made her both excited and scared at the same time, so she dropped her eyes away.

'No, you weren't.' He answered the question for her. 'You were lonely, or you were confused, or you were just plain curious. I don't know which. But you weren't willing… Not what I mean by it, anyway,' he said on a dry note, shaking his head at himself.

Kip made no reply. Perhaps she had been confused. She certainly was now. She had assigned Whitman Delaney the role of villain but he kept acting out of character.

'Come on.' He switched back to practicalities as he climbed out of the car and came round to open her door. He lifted her plastered leg onto the pavement while she swung her body round. 'How are we going to do this?'

'You could give me my crutches,' she suggested.

'Yeah, then what?' He looked pointedly towards the flights of steps that led up to the doors of all the houses on Washington Avenue. They were also several doors down from his father's house. 'How much practice have you had on these?' He nodded towards the steel walkers in the back of his car.

'None,' she admitted shortly.

'OK, so tomorrow you can be Miss Independence,' he said dismissively. 'Today we'll do it the easy way.'

He went round to the boot of the car and took out a folding wheelchair. Kip scowled at it. She'd used such to get around the hospital but she hadn't realised it would be going home with them.

He put an arm round her and lifted her carefully from the car into the chair. Then, instead of heading towards his father's house, he went the opposite way, rounding the end of the block before Kip caught on. There was no car access to the back of the houses but there was a path wide enough for a wheelchair. The back was level with the house so there were no steps, but it was still awkward to negotiate a narrow garden path glistening with December frost.

It took them five to ten minutes to reach the back door, and by then Kip appreciated two facts: one, that if you had to break your leg winter was not the best season to do it; and two, that she could never have managed her apartment steps.

Whit wheeled her into the kitchen where Alice Novak was baking.

Kip was surprised by the woman's concern. She had imagined that the older lady would resent her presence there, seeing her as a sponger, perhaps. But there was no hint of that as she expressed her sympathy at the accident and hustled Whit out of the way so that she could wheel Kip into the room she'd prepared.

It was at the back of the house, through from the kitchen, and had possibly been built as a housekeeper's room although Alice had never occupied it. Liking her independence, she kept up her own apartment, even though she spent much of her life at the Delaneys'.

The room was brighter than the rest of the house, with coral stripe and sky-blue wallpaper, blinds at the window and a freshness that suggested it had been recently painted.

Alice confirmed the latter as she said, 'The menfolk

wanted to do it up pink, but I reckoned you weren't the pink type.'

'I'm not.' Kip struggled to take in the fact that it had been decorated for her. No one, not even her father in their numerous moves, had ever done up a room specifically for her. 'It's lovely,' she added as Alice waited for her verdict.

'It's OK.' The older woman wasn't given to superlatives but looked pleased enough as she said, 'My nephew did it. Couldn't get anyone else, not with it being Christmas and all. Which reminds me, the professor apologises for not being here to welcome you. He'd promised Father Maloney to attend the carol service at St Joseph's.'

Carol service. Christmas. Four days away, it was one of Kip's major concerns. What was she going to do on a day that, above all, was a family day? She had no desire to intrude on their celebration.

'It's very professional.' She repeated her praise for the room before saying, 'Mrs Novak, about Christmas… Is there any chance of getting a taxi on Christmas Day?'

'A taxi?' Mrs Novak looked at her as if she were mad. 'What do you want a taxi for on Christmas? Oh, I see…' The older woman's expression cooled. 'A boyfriend, is it?'

'No, there's no boyfriend,' Kip denied soundly. 'It's just…well, Christmas is for families, and I'll only be in the way here… I thought I might spend the day at my apartment, clearing up.'

'Spend Christmas on your own?' Alice Novak was horrified.

Kip shrugged to show that she didn't mind. She'd spent several Christmases on her own; in fact, it had seemed almost a luxury compared to the uncertain Christmases with her father. How drunk would he be? When would he appear? Would he appear at all? Or, worse, would he be stone-cold sober and contrite, and make plans that would never come about, promising the earth only to snatch it away the very next day.

'I don't celebrate Christmas,' she declared finally.

Alice Novak's eyes narrowed on her. 'You're Jewish.'

Kip wasn't. She wasn't much of anything now, but what she had been was Methodist. It seemed easier, however, not to dispute the housekeeper's conclusion.

'Well, I don't suppose it'll matter to the professor what you are,' Alice Novak continued. 'He'll still be happy for you to sit down at his table Christmas Day. And it won't all be family, because I'll be there too.'

'You're sort of family,' Kip argued.

A small smile touched Alice Novak's lips at Kip's recognition of the fact, before she continued drily, 'And they need me to cook it too.'

'Well, I couldn't do that,' Kip sighed, and at Alice's frown explained, 'I can't cook.'

'Can't cook?' Alice was appalled.

Kip shook her head. She could boil an egg and open a can of beans and fry sausages, but there had been no one around to teach her more than these basics, and cooking skills had never seemed vital to her plans.

'I suppose you're one of those modern types—think cooking isn't going to catch you a man,' Alice stated reprovingly. 'Well, it might not catch one but it sure will keep one when the first fever's died down.'

At the risk of speaking sacrilege, Kip pointed out, 'I don't want to catch a man.'

'Huh!' Alice Novak gave one of her famous snorts. This one expressed disbelief. 'That's what you say now, but wait till you meet him—the one you can't live without. Then see how cool you are, missie,' she finished with a knowing air.

Kip stared at her in surprise. She hadn't expected someone as old or practical as Alice Novak to talk like some romantic novel.

'Look at me like that if you want—' Alice was astute enough to read her scepticism '—but mark my words. It comes to us all at least once in our lives.'

'Is that how you felt about Mr Novak?' Kip asked with a slight smile.

'Lord, no!' Alice denied unexpectedly. 'George Novak was a decent man, God rest his soul, but he wasn't one to inspire undying love… Boy before him broke my heart,' the old lady admitted in unusually reminiscent tones. 'Went off to Korea and died on me, wouldn't you know?'

'I…' Kip was taken aback and murmured an awkward 'I'm sorry.'

Alice shook her head. 'No need to be. It was forty years ago, child.' She dismissed any pain that lingered. 'Just warning you. It happens to us all. Even when you don't want it.'

Kip wondered if she was meant to be getting a message from all this. If she was, she was missing it.

She was relieved when Alice Novak returned to her normal, practical self, declaring, 'There's a toilet just down the corridor. You want some help, you call out.'

'Thanks,' Kip acknowledged, 'but I should be fine when I have my crutches.'

'Well, here's himself with them,' Mrs Novak announced as she passed Whit Delaney in the doorway of Kip's room.

He had her luggage too. He put the bag on the bed and came over with her crutches. 'How are you and Mrs Novak getting on?' he asked when the housekeeper had departed.

'Fine,' Kip felt able to say, then thought to add, 'I won't get in her way.'

'I wasn't worried about that,' he claimed. 'I was just curious… The two of you seemed to have a lot to say.'

'Not really,' Kip disclaimed, then a devil in her made her admit, 'Mrs Novak was just telling me about her love life.'

'Her what?' Whit wondered if he'd heard right.

'Her love life,' Kip repeated, before asking herself if this was the wisest topic to be discussing with him. She shook her head, deciding that explanations were too complicated.

Whit was still intrigued. 'Well, that's a challenge to the imagination—Alice Novak having a love life,' he drawled back.

Kip was stung on the other woman's behalf. 'She was young once.'

'Weren't we all?' Whit was now laughing at himself, adding, as he looked at her unlined face, 'Some of us still are… Twenty-one, isn't it?'

'Twenty-two,' she corrected him. 'I had a birthday.'

'When?'

'A few days ago.'

'You never said.' Whit frowned as he realised that there had been no one to mark it.

Kip shrugged. 'I don't celebrate birthdays,' she claimed seriously. 'In fact, I don't really celebrate Christmas either. So, if it's all right with you, I'll just stay in my room on Christmas Day.'

'It's all right with me,' he said with seeming indifference. 'Personally I think Christmas should be like the Olympics—once every four years.'

Kip felt a moment's relief. It was premature.

'Unfortunately,' he ran on, 'it won't be all right with my daughter, who thinks Christmas is the most wonderful day of the year—and for some reason considers your presence the icing on the cake. Nor with my father, who has invited you into his home and will feel deeply offended if you don't come to his table to celebrate Christmas with him... Still, it's up to you,' he added with a shrug.

The way he put it, Kip had no choice—no choice at all. She threw him a mutinous look, but he deflected it with a smile. A smile of triumph.

'Go away,' Kip muttered, but without much force.

'In a moment,' he agreed easily, 'when we see how you get on with the crutches.'

'I'll be fine.' Kip was confident that she could manage a pair of crutches, if not the rest of her life.

He didn't argue but said simply, 'Holler if you need anything,' before sauntering out of the room.

Kip decided that she would have to be dying before she shouted for his help. She had her pride.

But pride wasn't much good to her when she tried to get out of the wheelchair onto crutches. Pride didn't stop her from falling. Pride didn't stop her from crying in anger and frustration when she couldn't get herself up from the floor.

She didn't shout for Whit. He came, alerted by the sounds from her room.

He took in the scene: the abandoned wheelchair, the crutches and her lying at an angle on the floor, her face smudged with tears and temper and pain.

'I wanted the toilet,' she said in a small, pitiful voice that couldn't be hers.

'OK.' He read her no lecture but put his arm round her shoulders and lifted her to her feet—or at least one of them.

He supported her through to the toilet along the corridor and sat her on a chair placed sideways on to the pan. He left her to manage the rest. She called when she'd finished, and he helped her back to her room.

He saw the strain on her face, both physical and emotional, and guided her down onto the edge of the bed.

'Lie down,' he said simply, and lifted her plastered leg for her. He put a quilt over her and crossed to close her curtains. 'Sleep for a while.'

It was a measure of her tiredness that Kip didn't argue but did what he said. She slept. Not just for an hour or two but round the clock.

When she eventually woke it was to find Whitman Delaney sitting by her bed, watching her.

She opened her eyes and blinked the sleep out of them.

He smiled and, unguarded, she found herself smiling back.

He said nothing, but stood and briefly touched her hand before walking out of the room.

A sense of unreality gripped Kip. It was as if she was in a fairy story. The princess slept for a hundred years until the handsome prince appeared to release her from the spell.

It was only later that Kip realised how wrong she was and that that was probably the moment she'd fallen *under* Whitman Delaney's spell. And, by the time she understood that, it was far too late.

CHAPTER SEVEN

KIP had never experienced jealousy before. It took her by surprise. She glanced towards Whit and Faye Gilbert, laughing together at the New Year's party, and her stomach went into a clutch of knots.

Abby followed the direction of her eyes. 'Faye used to be his girlfriend when he lived in New York. If you don't like her, that's OK. I don't like her either.'

Kip quickly masked her expression from the child. 'I don't know her.'

'Well, take it from me,' Abby sighed expressively, 'you don't want to.'

'What's wrong with her?' Kip couldn't resist asking.

'Well...' Abby looked as if it was hard to pick out one thing and finally settled on a comprehensive 'Everything.'

Kip didn't take her opinion too seriously. She understood the child better now. In the short time that she'd been at the Delaneys Abby had been her shadow. She didn't mind. It had got her through Christmas Day; unable to help Mrs Novak with any of the preparations, she'd felt less of a lame duck by playing with Abby.

Kip didn't flatter herself as to the reason for her sudden popularity with the child. Abby was lonely. Kip recognised the symptoms from her own childhood.

'Why don't you go and play with the others?' Kip felt it was wrong for Abby to spend the whole party in the corner with her.

Alex Delaney always had a get-together on New Year's Eve for friends and family, and, with his doctor's approval, he'd gone ahead as usual. Mostly the company consisted of his older colleagues at the college, but there were one or two couples with young children that Abby could play with. And Whit, of course, had Faye Gilbert.

Abby screwed up her face at Kip's suggestion. 'Don't want to. They laugh at me.'

'Why?' Kip frowned.

'Don't know.' Abby shrugged.

Because she was different, Kip guessed, and her heart went out to the child. Abby was a mixture of high intelligence and eccentricity. Kip thought her a very rewarding child, but other kids possibly wouldn't appreciate the fact.

'Can I stay with you?' Abby added, down in the mouth.

'Of course you can,' Kip assured her. 'I just don't want you to feel you have to look after me all the time.'

It was the right thing to say. For all her apparent confidence, Abby was uncertain of her role in a household geared towards the adults. She needed to feel some sense of importance.

'It's OK,' she said, as if bestowing a favour, 'I'll stay. I mean, it wouldn't be right, leaving you alone. You don't know anyone, do you?'

'Not really, no.'

'Well, there you are, then.' Abby settled the matter and leaned a little closer to Kip on the old armchair they shared.

They were sitting like that, heads close, when Whit Delaney noticed them. For a moment their closeness made him smile. Then he thought about it, and wondered if it was especially wise to encourage Abby's fondness for Kip.

He left Faye in discussion with a lecturer from media studies. 'Can I get you girls something?'

'I'll have a white wine,' Abby piped up with a grin as cheeky as you please.

'A lemonade, right,' Whit agreed. 'And you, Kipling? There's Mrs Novak's punch—a fairly lethal concoction—or would you prefer wine?'

Kip shook her head. 'I don't drink,' she said simply.

It was Abby who claimed extravagantly, 'Kip's an athlete. Her body's a temple.'

'Really?' Whit raised a brow at his daughter's announcement. 'Well, far be it from me to set her on the road to ruin… Can I get you something to eat, or would that be defiling the temple too?' he asked with irony.

A dull flush crept up on Kip's face. His joke had made her think of the time they'd been together in her apartment.

'I'm not hungry,' she mumbled back.

'Kip has to watch what she eats.' Abby spoke up for her again. 'I mean, it's all right for people like Miss Gilbert. She can get as fat as she likes. But Kip has to stay in shape.'

Abby was speaking off the top of her own head, not Kip's.

Fortunately Whit knew his daughter well enough to realise it. 'Abby,' he said very quietly, 'remember what I asked you earlier about Faye?'

'I…yes.' Now it was Abby's turn to flush a dull red.

'Well, please try,' he added, and took any sting out of his words by leaning down and planting a kiss on his daughter's cheek. 'I'll go get your lemonade…and one for you, Kipling?'

Kip nodded, and they both watched his retreating back.

Abby looked guilty rather than resentful as she admitted, 'He asked me to be nice to Miss Gilbert. I promised but then I forgot. Do you think he's in love with her?' Abby added, much to Kip's consternation.

'I—I… I don't know about these things,' she eventually replied.

'He could be,' Abby decided. 'I think she is with him. That's why she keeps trying to be nice to me. She knows my dad wouldn't want her if she was nasty to me…but I don't reckon she really likes me.'

'You don't know that.' From what Kip had seen, Faye Gilbert was an intelligent, attractive woman who had been perfectly pleasant to the child.

Abby gave her a look that asked whose side she was on.

The child was too young to appreciate the fact that Kip was very much on *her* side. It would have been easy for Kip to rubbish Faye Gilbert—to see the woman's charm as phoney and her beauty as artificial—but if Whit Delaney was

serious about her it was going to be vitally important for
Abby to learn to like the woman.

'I think you should give her a chance,' Kip added carefully.

'Why?' Abby countered, still feeling contrary.

'Because it's the smart thing to do,' Kip stated matter-of-
factly.

She didn't see Whit Delaney standing before them with
their glasses in his hands.

'What is?' He glanced from one face to another.

'Nothing,' they answered simultaneously, drawing a
frown.

'Very conspiratorial.' His voice was dry but his eyes were
worried.

Abby was unfazed. 'What does con-spir-tral mean?'

'Con-spir-a-torial,' he repeated for her benefit. 'It means
you and Kipling are planning something in secret.'

They hadn't been—not really—but they still looked guilty
and their silence seemed to speak volumes.

'Never mind.' He handed them a lemonade each and said
as a parting shot, 'I'll get the thumbscrews out later.'

'Is he cross with us or joking?' Abby was uncertain of her
father's reaction.

So was Kip, but she assured the child with some confidence, 'He won't be cross with you, pet.'

Kip had yet to see Whit Delaney get angry with his daughter. Even when she was being difficult he was firm rather
than furious. Kip suspected that it was *her* apparent influence
over his daughter that concerned him.

Kip watched as he rejoined Faye Gilbert, who smiled up
at him, her feelings plain. They were probably reciprocated
too, because he put an arm around her.

Jealousy was a physical pain somewhere between her ribs
and her heart. It drove Kip to hobble to her room the moment
Abby went upstairs to bed.

The party itself went on for several hours more, until grad-
ually the house quietened and the last guest left. Alex Delaney knocked on her door to check that she was all right,

before retiring. She didn't hear Whit at all, although usually she did, moving about downstairs after the rest had gone to bed. Tonight, she assumed, he was with Faye Gilbert.

Sleepless, Kip decided to get up and make herself a drink. She was now quite adept at moving around. She didn't bother dressing but left on the long T-shirt that she used as a nightgown. She hobbled through to the kitchen and, with some effort, managed to boil milk for cocoa. She perched on a bar stool to drink it.

She looked around the room where they normally sat for meals, and reflected on the last ten days. Living with the Delaneys had proved surprisingly *un*traumatic. She'd assumed that it would be a burden for the family, having a stranger in their midst, but Professor Delaney and Abby had behaved as if her presence was an unexpected bonus: for the professor, a young mind to train; for Abby, someone to play with.

Kip could have been happy too but for the one member of the household who had a problem with her being there. Whit Delaney. He hadn't said as much. He could hardly do so, when it was he who had insisted that she come there. But that was penance, not liking, and, on the few occasions they'd found themselves alone together, he hadn't talked to her but had watched her with a troubled eye. Perhaps he'd worried that she might misunderstand and interpret any sort of overture to her as personal interest.

Was that why he had produced Faye Gilbert—to discourage Kip? Certainly she had appeared like a rabbit out of a hat. His father had looked surprised when he'd announced that the woman was coming to stay for a couple of days, and Alice Novak had mumbled about no warning and clearing out an upstairs boxroom, before Whit had assured them that Miss Gilbert would be quite content staying at a hotel.

Kip would have felt guilty about occupying the spare bedroom if she hadn't realised the obvious: Whit Delaney wanted this woman in a hotel room—a hotel room he could visit without his father or daughter in the vicinity.

Kip guessed that he was there now. Sleeping. No, *not* sleeping.

She shut her eyes. She didn't want to imagine him with Faye Gilbert. It made her feel sick with jealousy.

It was a shock to feel anything so strongly. She had always believed herself immune to such emotions.

She opened her eyes and got another shock, as a dark figure passed by the kitchen window. Her first thought was of burglars, before a key scraped in the lock.

He came through the back door, his dark blond hair coated with snow. He shook it off and turned to lock up before he noticed her sitting in shadow.

He seemed disconcerted for a moment, but recovered quickly enough as he came to lean against the work surface beside her.

'Waiting up for me? I'm touched,' he drawled, in a slightly mocking tone that set Kip's teeth on edge.

'Of course not!' she snapped in reply. 'I didn't think you'd *be* back!'

If anything, his smile became more mocking. 'Why? Where did you think I'd be?'

With Faye Gilbert, of course, but Kip wasn't about to say so. This man might hold some inexplicable attraction for her, but she refused to play his silly games. She scowled in return and made to pick up her crutches.

He got there first and placed them out of her reach. 'You're not going to pull your usual disappearing act, are you?'

Kip had been about to do just that. She didn't trust him in this mood. She sensed that anger lay beneath the mockery.

'I'm quite safe, you know.' He looked anything but as he smiled lazily.

'Safe?' she echoed, though she understood well enough.

It was no discouragement. He spelled out, 'Even at the extremes of sexual frustration, I make it a point of honour never to ravage women wearing plaster casts.'

She began to protest. 'I didn't think—'

'Didn't you?' A brow lifted in disbelief. 'You jump out of your skin any time I'm near. Sometimes I think I should make a move on you just to get it over with. Then you could slap my face or tell me to go to hell or whatever, and I could stop feeling like I had the leper's touch.'

'That's not true.' Kip didn't think that way. 'I don't expect... I know it was a one-time thing—you and me. You don't have to fend me off with ex-girlfriends,' she added in an angry rush.

He looked surprised. 'Is that what I'm doing?' He laughed—a humourless sound. 'You don't know much about men, do you?'

'I've never claimed to,' she threw back, then could have bitten her tongue off as jealousy prompted her to say, 'I suppose Faye does.'

'Faye?' he echoed, as if the woman had momentarily slipped his mind.

Kip assumed that they'd gone back to playing games and reminded him heavily, 'The woman you were with tonight.'

His eyes narrowed on her face before he answered her, 'Yes, you could say Faye knows the score. That's why women like Faye are right for me.'

And, presumably, women—or girls—like Kip weren't. Well, it was hardly news, but it hurt all the same.

'Could you please hand me my crutch?' she said in the steadiest voice she could manage.

Only it wasn't very steady. There was a catch in it that betrayed some of her confusion of feelings.

'In a moment,' he agreed, but though he straightened from the worktop it was to sit on the chair by her side. He took her hand and held onto it when she would have pulled it away. 'Kipling, we're going to have to come to terms with this thing between us, otherwise it's going to be impossible round here. My father might seem well but his doctor has insisted he doesn't go back to work for at least another semester. That means I'm going to be here for another three to four months minimum.'

What was he saying? What was he asking of her? Kip wasn't certain.

'I won't be here that long,' she countered. 'My cast comes off in a month.'

'And then what?' He looked at her with pity.

It was worse than scorn. 'I can get on with my life,' she retorted, grabbing her hand from his.

'Intent on the path to glory?' he asked, a sigh in his voice.

Kip wasn't sure how she felt about athletics any more. It had been five weeks since she'd run, but it seemed longer. It was as if she'd got off a treadmill and didn't know if she wanted to get on again.

She still scowled back at him. 'What's wrong with that?'

'Nothing, provided it doesn't mean excluding everything else,' he stated, concern now in his steady blue gaze. 'There has to be more to life than running.'

Not for Kip there wasn't. 'Like what?' she flipped back.

His mouth twisted. 'I don't know. Hobbies. Your studies... Boys,' he suggested tentatively.

Boys? Kip glared at him. Oh, she understood him. She understood him only too well. He wanted to fix her up with some stupid, spotty-faced youth so that he could absolve himself of any guilt when he swanned off with his lady-friend.

'OK, if that's what you want,' she retorted airily, 'I'll sleep with the entire athletics team. That way I can combine my training with my social life, and you can be happy in the knowledge that you've rescued me from a sterile existence.'

Whit Delaney had never hit a woman but he came close to hitting one now. She was so difficult. No, she was god-damn impossible. He was only trying to... What *was* he trying to do?

He asked himself the question and answered it in the same breath. She was right, of course. That was what made him mad—that she saw through him. He *was* trying to clear his conscience.

He watched her closely but had no real idea of what was going on in her head. She seemed genuinely indifferent. Perhaps he was the only one who had a problem letting go of that night in her apartment.

'Fine!' he growled in reply, and handed her her crutches.

He stood clear as she levered herself to her feet. She managed it without his help but then overbalanced. He caught and steadied her, his hands round her waist.

She flushed at the contact, declaring tensely, 'I'm OK.'

He kept hold of her. He could feel the warmth of her skin under the T-shirt she wore. She still shivered at his touch. Her eyes lifted to his—an opaque green that refused to reveal her secrets.

He didn't plan it, but he didn't control it either. He wanted to kiss her. He had to kiss her, to see if the last time had been madness or something all too real.

His lips came down on hers before she had time to turn her head away. At first she resisted, her mouth closed against his, but he kept kissing her, driven by compulsion and need. Then it was as he remembered—the taste of her, the smell, the sound, his breath or hers quickening with that sudden rush of desire.

One crutch fell with a clattering noise onto the tiled floor, but he didn't let her go. Instead he gathered her close and pulled her down with him on a low chair, still kissing her. She did not resist. Perhaps she couldn't. He held her on his knee with one arm while he touched her with the other—her face, her neck, her breasts, finding their fullness beneath the thin cotton of her nightshirt, needing more.

The T-shirt was already pushed up over her thighs. It was too easy to push it further, to slide his hand over her narrow hips to her back, and round, to cup the soft, damp flesh of her breasts. The nipples were already hard before he brushed his fingers against them, and she moaned in her throat as his tongue thrust inside her mouth.

He felt his body harden. He wanted her there and then. He wanted to draw her down on the kitchen floor and cover her body with his. He wanted to lose himself inside her. But the very strength of his desire shocked and sobered him. It hadn't been a moment's madness. He had to stop now, or he wouldn't be able to.

He dragged his mouth from hers and stood up, slipping her off his lap. He'd forgotten all about her leg. He heard

her cry out with pain. He grabbed her before she could fall
and carefully set her down on the chair. He saw that she was
white and shaken.

'Are you OK?' He wondered if he'd damaged her leg.

She nodded, but didn't lift her head.

'I'm sorry. I shouldn't have,' he ran on. 'I don't know
what came over me.'

It sounded a pathetic excuse, even to his own ears. It was
hardly a surprise that her mouth twisted in derision. She said
nothing. Her eyes said more, as she stared at the kitchen
floor. She was angry with him and ashamed of herself.

Kip tried believing that he had forced her, but it didn't
work. She could still hear her heart hammering with excitement. She still had the taste of him in her mouth. She still
felt the rough sensuality of his hands on her skin, and recalled
the promise of pleasure his touch had brought. She knew that,
once again, she hadn't been the one to withdraw.

But her anger made her lash out, demanding, 'Isn't one
woman a night enough for you?'

He shook his head. 'I haven't made love to Faye—not
tonight, anyway,' he stated with a ring of truth.

Was that meant to make Kip feel better? 'I suppose you
respect *her* too much,' she spat at him.

He answered quietly, 'I respect you.'

'Like hell!' Kip didn't want his well-meant lies. She
placed a hand on the table to lever herself up.

He gripped her wrist, preventing her. 'Why do you think
I stopped? I wanted you. You must know that.'

Kip stared at him in reply. She didn't know what she knew
any more. How could she want a man and not even be very
sure if she liked him? She didn't trust her *own* feelings, far
less his. It seemed easier to be his enemy.

'Wouldn't she let you, then?' she scoffed, fired by her
jealousy of Faye Gilbert.

'Forget Faye!' he dismissed. 'It's you and I that have to
learn to live together, if only for my father's sake. He doesn't
need any kind of stress.'

Kip's anger changed to resentment. 'Do you think I'd do anything to hurt your father?'

He shook his head. 'Not deliberately, no—but any tension in the house is bound to affect him. That's why we need to have a truce.'

'A truce?' Kip was instantly suspicious. Truce or surrender? *Her* surrender.

'I promise not to touch you again, you stop treating me like something contagious,' he suggested in a totally serious vein, 'and we'll work from there. What do you say?'

He made it sound easy. Perhaps for him it was. He might have started things but he'd also called a halt. He had always been in control.

'I mean it. I won't touch you again,' he repeated in the face of her lengthening silence.

Kip believed him. She knew that he already regretted touching her this time.

'All right.' She nodded in agreement.

'Good.' He held her hand briefly, then released it.

It was over, Kip realised, so why was there no relief, only that feeling that another door in her life had just slammed shut?

'Are you OK?' He saw the shadows in her eyes.

'My ankle hurts.' Kip focused on her physical pain. It was easier to deal with.

'I'll get your tablets.' He rose and went through to her bedroom, returning with her painkillers.

He fetched a glass of water and Kip swallowed the pills down before reaching for her crutches.

He handed them to her. 'Do you want some help?'

'No, thanks.' Kip rose carefully to her feet, this time without mishap.

She limped towards the door and did not turn as he called out, 'Goodnight, Kip.'

'Goodnight,' she echoed, before slipping inside her bedroom, wishing now that she had never left it.

It was like a sickness, the way he made her feel. One

moment she was strong and angry and in control, the nex
she was weak and dizzy and incapable of thought. Just a kiss
and her will dissolved.

It *was* a sickness. What else could it be?

CHAPTER EIGHT

IF THE TRUCE had relied on Kip, it would never have been reached. She woke the next morning still feeling awkward and angry round Whit, mumbling in monosyllables or seething in silence.

She was like a bad-tempered child, too tired and too upset to know what she wanted. And, though she didn't see it at the time that was exactly how Whit treated her—as a child whose tantrums were ignored or tolerated because they were an expression of the hurt inside. A child who needed humouring rather than punishing for the dark moods that sometimes smothered her.

Whit put up with it all. He never lost his temper. He confined disapproval to a look of disappointment.

It was almost impossible to rage against such reasonableness, but Kip tried. She spent a lot of time trying.

She was glad when college recommenced. He went back to work while she remained at home, studying with his father. That meant that he was out of the house from morning to early evening.

The down side was Stacey. She reappeared to babysit Abby.

Abby protested that she didn't need Stacey. She had Kip now, but her father pointed out that Kip wasn't sufficiently mobile to look after a cantankerous eight-year-old.

He made it seem as if his consideration was for Kip, but Kip doubted it. He still didn't want her around his daughter too much. He preferred Stacey; perhaps he really did believe that she was the pleasant, smiling Barbie doll she appeared.

Naturally Stacey didn't waste her charm on Kip, greeting her with a blunt, 'I hear you've been crippled for life.'

'That's a lie!' was screamed back at her by Abby.

Kip was too busy wondering who had told her that. Whit, she supposed.

The girl ignored Abby, smiling slyly, 'Still, there's always the paraplegics' Olympics. You can enter the one-legged race.'

'Shut up!' Again it was Abby that shouted her down. 'I'll tell my dad if you don't.'

'Go ahead; he won't believe you.' Stacey was confident. Abby had already told too many false stories against her.

'He'll believe Kip,' Abby claimed. 'Won't he, Kip?'

Kip doubted it. 'Leave it, Abby. It doesn't matter.'

'Very sensible, *Kip*,' Stacey crowed back. 'Otherwise I might have to tell the professor just why poor little Orphan Annie chose to step off the sidewalk in the first place.'

Kip frowned, not sure what Stacey was getting at.

'What do you mean?' was demanded of her by Abby.

Stacey looked hugely pleased with herself. Kip had a premonition of what was coming and said to Abby, 'Stacey's just fooling around… Listen, Abby, could you possibly go get me a glass of water from the kitchen? I've got an awful thirst.'

Abby looked frustrated. She didn't want to leave the conversation, but she didn't feel that she could ignore Kip's request either. Reluctantly she trooped off to the kitchen, leaving Kip and Stacey alone together in the lounge.

Kip didn't waste any time. 'So, enlighten me, why did I step off the sidewalk?'

'Miss High and Mighty,' Stacey sneered at Kip's haughty tone. 'But you won't be, when I tell the professor the truth. You see, I know someone who was there, the day you were knocked down. He was right behind you and saw the lot. In fact he picked up your handbag…'

Stacey paused for dramatic effect. Kip had a sinking feeling in her stomach.

'The contents had scattered over the sidewalk,' Stacey continued, and listed, 'Pens, notes, pocketbook, comb...' before getting to the punchline '...pregnancy test.'

Kip visibly blanched. Stacey smiled in satisfaction.

Kip decided to brazen it out. 'So what?'

'So who's the father?' Stacey flipped back.

'I'm not pregnant,' Kip stated bluntly, hoping to kill the subject dead.

'Not now, no,' Stacey conceded. 'I guess stepping into the path of an oncoming car is a sure-fire form of abortion.'

'I was *never* pregnant,' Kip stressed angrily.

'You expect me to believe that?' Stacey gave a derisive laugh.

'I don't care what you believe,' Kip countered.

'No? Well, maybe we should see if the professor cares,' Stacey added menacingly, 'what with you living in his house and all.'

'You've no reason to bother him about this.' Kip struggled to keep her temper. 'He hasn't been well, remember.'

Stacey frowned, then realised that they were talking at cross purposes. 'Not the old prof. Who cares what he thinks? But Whitman—that's another story. Will he want a nympho-maniac with no scruples round his precious little princess? Somehow I don't think so.'

Kip kept her cool and returned, 'In that case, perhaps *you* should consider handing in your notice.'

'What?' Stacey took a second or two to catch on. 'I wasn't talking about me!'

'Weren't you?' Kip feigned innocence.

'You know I wasn't,' Stacey hissed back. 'And you'll be laughing on the other side of your face when I tell the pro-fessor.'

'Go ahead, tell him.' Kip's indifference was genuine.

'Tell me what?' a third voice interjected from the doorway.

Whit was standing there, glass in hand. He must have in-tercepted Abby on her way back from the kitchen. There was no sign of the child.

'Tell me what?' he repeated at their silence.

'Oh, Professor!' A half-sob in her voice, Stacey crossed

the room to him. 'I didn't really want to say anything, but there's all sorts of rumours going round college.'

'Rumours?' His eyes went to Kip.

She shook her head before he jumped to any wrong conclusions.

Stacey gushed on, 'About Kip's accident and what caused it, and, well, about…' She trailed off as if delicacy inhibited her from saying more.

'About me?' Whit suggested.

It drew a puzzled look from Stacey and a positive glare from Kip.

Kip leapt in smartly, 'About whether you should let me hang round Abby, considering. You see, Sherlock Holmes here—' she cast a disparaging glance at Stacey '—has discovered I did a pregnancy test just before my accident, and she thinks I flung myself under a car rather than face the consequences. It's rot, of course. I wasn't pregnant and, even if I had been, the *boy* and I would have worked something out.'

'I see.' He gave her an odd look. It should have been gratitude but it wasn't.

'What boy?' Stacey demanded immediately. Perhaps she'd sensed an air of invention round Kip's story.

'No one special. Someone I met at an athletics meet a while ago,' Kip answered with suitable vagueness.

'You don't have to say anything more,' Whit put in. 'I don't believe any of this is Stacey's concern.'

Stacey looked resentful. 'I was just trying to protect Abby from bad influence,' she intoned piously.

'Bad influence being anyone who has sex outside marriage?' Whit raised a mocking brow. 'Well, that surely includes a large section of the adult population. What do you suggest? That I demand my daughter's companions all prove they're *virgo intacta*. I believe that's the correct medical expression.'

'*Professor!* Really!' Stacey was shocked by his explicitness.

'Personally, I think that's a mite drastic,' he continued urbanely, 'but if you wish to volunteer for such a test—'

'Of course not!' This time Stacey looked positively alarmed. 'I mean—not that I have anything to hide. I'm not the one doing pregnancy tests,' she added, with a disparaging glance at Kip.

'Quite,' he conceded. 'I'm sure you're well ahead of the game in that respect.'

'I... What?' Stacey didn't know if she'd been insulted or complimented.

While she made up her mind Whit went on, 'Still, I can see you're not happy with the situation, and that leaves me in something of a dilemma. Do I retain your services and throw Kipling out on the streets, injury notwithstanding? Or do I ignore the rumours, offend your sensibilities and reluctantly accept your resignation? On balance, I think it'll have to be the latter.'

'What?' Stacey was still trying to catch up with events. They certainly weren't going as she'd planned.

'I will, of course, recompense you for injured feelings.' He went into his jacket pocket and drew out a cheque-book.

Both girls watched as he wrote out a cheque, leaning on the doorframe. Stacey fumed visibly. Kip repressed a rogue desire to laugh.

'There you go.' He handed Stacey the cheque. 'Naturally I shall count on your discretion.'

Stacey was livid with embarrassed anger until she read the amount, then her face went through a range of expression before greed won out. 'I...yes, I don't gossip... And you really don't have to do this,' she added, possibly recalling that her English grades depended on this man.

'No, I don't,' he agreed, 'but I don't want there to be any bad feelings round your departure.'

'Not on my part, Professor,' she assured him eagerly.

'Good.' He smiled tightly. 'I'll show you out.'

'No, it's OK, I know the way.' Stacey smiled back, seemingly still attracted, before sliding Kip a look of total dislike.

Kip waited just long enough for Stacey to shut the outside door, then demanded, 'How much did you give her?'

'Enough,' he answered succinctly.

'You shouldn't have given her anything,' Kip told him crossly.

'I didn't want her bad-mouthing you round college,' he replied, 'especially if I'm the cause.'

'I wasn't going to tell her about you,' Kip insisted.

'No, and I'm grateful.' His eyes rested on her face.

'Don't be!' Kip didn't want his gratitude. 'I was protecting myself as much as you.'

His mouth twisted. 'Presumably it's preferable to be known for indulging in casual sex with a stranger rather than admit having an affair with your English professor... I suppose kids your age think anyone over thirty-five is geriatric territory.'

'Practically,' she agreed, resenting his reference to her as a kid.

'Ouch,' he grimaced, but without any real dent in his confidence.

Why should there be? He must know how attractive he was. Up to this point Stacey had all but thrown herself at him.

'On that note,' he went on, 'I think I'll go relay the good news to Abby. She's been trying to get rid of Stacey since day one.'

'I'm not surprised,' Kip muttered under her breath.

He still caught it, claiming, 'She seemed OK to me.'

'I'm sure she did.' Kip did an only slightly exaggerated version of Stacey, fluttering her eyelids and simpering, '"Oh, Pwofessor, I just adore your little girl. Such a sweetie-pie I could eat her all up."'

'I guess she was a little over the top,' he admitted. 'But she seemed genuinely fond of Abby—more than Abby deserved, at any rate.'

Kip gave a snort of disbelief. '"Fond" is not the word,' she said, then added drily, 'Try irritated, uninterested, intolerant...'

His brows drew together. 'Why didn't you tell me all this?'

'You would have believed me, would you?' Kip challenged him.

'As a matter of fact, I would,' he answered. 'I've always found you quite ruthless with the truth.'

Kip glared. 'I don't believe in dressing things up, if that's what you mean.'

'Probably.' He smiled at her grumpy expression, as Abby reappeared.

'Where's Stacey?' the child asked.

'Gone to a better place,' he answered briefly, and was awarded a face-splitting grin.

'Great.' Abby didn't hide her delight. 'Does that mean Kip can be my babysitter now?'

'Forget it,' he advised. 'Kip's still recuperating.'

His concern appeared to be for Kip, but she suspected that it was just an excuse. He didn't trust her.

'Well, I don't want another one,' Abby protested. 'I can look after myself. It's not like Stacey did anything, anyway, 'cept file her nails and watch TV.'

'She took you out to the movies once or twice,' he reminded her.

'Only so she could suck face with her boyfriend,' Abby countered smartly.

Whit looked surprised, then appalled. 'Where did you get that awful expression? And don't say my books. May I be electrocuted by my word processor before I write such a thing.'

'A girl called Binkie in my class,' Abby related. 'Her mother's always sucking face with the boy who mows their lawn.'

Whit still looked mildly horrified. 'The sooner we go home the better. For now, perhaps you could select your friends with slightly more judgement.'

'I don't have any friends,' Abby announced sorrowfully. 'Only Kip. And she's a good influence on me, aren't you, Kip?'

Put on the spot, Kip remained silent.

'Modesty forbids Kipling from commenting,' Whit stated drily, 'but she certainly does seem to have a calming effect on you. It's just a pity she's incapacitated.'

He sounded sincere and Kip found herself saying, 'I couldn't fetch her from school, but I could mind her afterwards, if you like.'

'There!' Abby exclaimed with satisfaction. 'And you could pay her money because she hasn't got any.'

'*Abby!*' Kip and Whit reproved her simultaneously.

Then Whit added, 'I'm sorry. I should have thought.'

'It doesn't matter.' Kip's voice was stiff with pride.

'I'd still pay you,' he insisted, 'if you could look after her for a couple of hours in the afternoon.'

Kip nodded. 'Till my cast's removed.'

'What happens then?' Abby piped up.

There was a moment's silence between the adults before Whit came up with, 'Then she might choose to get as far away as possible from anyone with the name Delaney.'

He smiled to show that he was joking. Kip managed a slight smile back. It hid her real thoughts.

Soon her cast would be removed and she would no longer have a reason to stay at Washington Avenue, and she dreaded the day. It had been a mistake coming here, living with the Delaneys, because now she couldn't imagine living without them. Not just Abby and the old professor, but this man too.

When had that happened? When had he become so important to her?

'Perhaps if we're really, really nice to her, Daddy,' Abby suggested brightly, 'she'll never want to leave.'

'Perhaps,' Whit echoed, catching Kip's eyes as he added with a soft laugh, 'And if that doesn't work we could always make her our prisoner.'

Kip blushed deeply, aware that he was flirting with her, too tongue-tied to respond.

It was Abby who said fancifully, 'Like a princess in an ivory tower. You'd have to grow your hair long so the prince could rescue you.'

'Ah, but what if it's the prince who's captured her,' Whit continued in the same vein, 'only she doesn't realise it yet?'

Now his eyes contained a message, but Kip was too scared of her own feelings to read it.

'What do you think, Kip?' Abby appealed when she remained silent.

'I think…you're both as silly as each other,' she dismissed, purposely brisk. 'And I'll settle for being babysitter, thank you.'

'Spoken like a proper English nanny—obviously made for the job,' Whit remarked at her prim and proper tone, then was wise enough to change the subject.

Kip was left embarrassed but pleased. It sat easier with her pride to have a useful role in the household.

She was surely an unlikely choice, however. She knew little about how eight-year-olds should behave and was hardly in a position to run after Abby if she was naughty.

Fortunately, having got her own way, Abby adopted the role of model child—especially when her father was present—and he appeared satisfied with the arrangement.

Kip still found it hard to act naturally when he was around. She was polite and almost docile by her own standards, but she resisted any overtures to put them on a more friendly footing. She didn't want to be his friend. She didn't want to get to like him.

She tried reminding him of their real relationship by calling him 'Professor', ignoring his suggestions that she use his first name. Yet she resented it when he played the role of teacher, commenting on the work she'd submitted for her course credits.

Not that his comments were negative. One evening, while she was studying with his father, Whit returned an essay to her with a grade A, saying that her progress was quite remarkable. Her literacy now equalled the standard of most students, while her perception went far beyond.

Kip didn't know how to react. She wasn't used to praise. She questioned if it was genuine. Alex Delaney obviously believed that it was, and expressed his own satisfaction. Kip remained silent. She was still trapped in emotional illiteracy.

The men went on to discuss her potential and Kip realised then that that was all she was to them—a pet project. But what else had she expected? She should have been grateful to them for bothering. She had no reason to feel resentment. She just did.

She excused herself and went to the kitchen to make coffee.

Whit tracked her down there a few minutes later. 'What's wrong, Kip?'

What could she say? I don't want your praise and condescension? I don't want to be just one of your students? I want— She stopped her thoughts dead.

'Nothing!' she said aloud.

'Are you feeling OK?' There was concern in his voice.

Kip could have screamed. His consideration was killing her.

She snapped instead, 'Fine! Couldn't be better. A hundred per cent—except for a bloody great cast at the end of my leg.'

It just gave him another chance to be exasperatingly patient. 'Never mind. Your cast should be removed next week.'

'And that'll make everything hunky-dory, will it?' Kip was cross with herself now, as well as with him.

'No.' His eyes rested on her face but he seemed to look beyond. 'It's going to be a long road back. I guess you're a little frightened,' he added quietly.

'*Frightened!*' Kip's mood went from dark to black. 'Why should I be frightened?' she demanded furiously.

'I would be.' His tone remained calm. 'I would be scared of that twenty-five per cent chance.'

'Well, I'm not,' she retorted, putting on a brave front.

It was the same brave front that she'd been adopting since her last hospital appointment. Whit had driven her up to Boston and assumed the right to be in on her consultation. For the first time the surgeon had told her straight: there was a possibility that the foot would remain dysfunctional.

Kip hadn't followed the medical explanation but she'd reached the bottom line quickly enough. There was a one in four chance that her foot would remain useless and still require amputation.

Whit had tried to speak to her about it on the way home but she'd turned away and stared out of the window, and, if he'd seen the tears running down her face, he had kept mercifully silent.

He stayed silent now, but Kip could feel his eyes on her, watching, waiting. For what?

'I won't fall apart.' She answered the question she read in those steady blue eyes.

He didn't deny it, but said instead, 'Would falling apart be so bad? Release is sometimes healthier than suppression.'

'When I need to hire an analyst, I'll rob a bank, thank you,' Kip retorted smartly.

He laughed, genuinely amused. 'In other words, mind my own business.'

'Something like that,' Kip agreed, but without force. His laughter had disarmed her.

'Fair enough.' He inclined his head, accepting her right to the privacy of her thoughts, then added, 'About your essay— I meant what I said. It was seriously good.'

'Thanks.' This time Kip flushed with pleasure at his praise. 'I've never had an A in my life before.'

'Well, you can't thank me for that.' He smiled back. 'One of the other professors graded it.'

Kip frowned. 'I don't understand.'

'I read through the essay and was immediately impressed,' he explained. 'However, I didn't want to risk any accusations of bias, so I handed it over to a colleague. He has no idea of your background and judged it purely on merit.'

'Really?' Kip didn't hide her satisfaction.

Whit observed the difference. 'What did you think earlier—that I'd marked it up because it was you?'

'I...no, not exactly.' Kip bit her lip. She couldn't tell him how hard she found it to accept a pupil-teacher relationship with him.

'Well, I might have,' he admitted drily. 'That's why I bumped it elsewhere.'

'Oh.' Kip was surprised by his honesty. She made the mistake of looking at him directly.

His eyes caught and held hers and conveyed the compassion he felt for her. It made the breath catch in Kip's throat. No one had ever cared for her like this. It might be pity, but it was real and deep.

It was then that she realised how unreasonable her own behaviour was. Whit was right. She was scared—scared of so many things that she wouldn't even admit it to herself. Instead she'd blamed Whit, for anything and everything.

'I'm sorry,' she said inadequately.

'Sorry? Sorry for what?' He gave her a quizzical smile.

She shook her head. She couldn't explain, not properly. Instead she bluntly admitted, 'I've been a complete cow!'

His brows lifted at the confession and he laughed briefly, before realising that she was being serious. 'No, you haven't,' he returned quietly.

'I have!' she insisted, as fierce as ever.

Whit decided that it was probably wisest not to argue. 'All right, if you say so.'

Kip pulled a face, muttering another 'Sorry.'

'Don't worry about it.' He was used to her uncertain temper. 'Still, I think I'll quit while I'm ahead,' he added, going towards the door. 'Goodnight, Kip.'

'Goodnight, Whit.' His name slipped out quite naturally—the first time she'd ever used it.

Whit stopped dead in the doorway, and turned to look at her. She seemed as surprised as he was. But he had the sense not to comment, just smiling slightly before he went off down the corridor.

Kip realised then what she'd been denying for months. She'd kept Whit Delaney at a distance, not out of anger or contempt, but because she was afraid—afraid that she might grow to like him, afraid that she might like him too much.

It was so much simpler, safer to see him as a villain, an older man who had carelessly seduced then discarded her.

But he kept slipping out of character, being someone else—someone that it was hard to put easy labels on. If it had been a careless moment, that evening in her apartment, then he had surely paid for it many times over.

And hadn't it been her madness too? She hadn't stopped him. She hadn't even tried. She hadn't at New Year either. He had been the one to call a halt before the situation spiralled out of control.

So why was she blaming him, punishing him? Was it for the seduction or for the rejection later?

Kip closed her mind to the question, but some of her anger with him still slipped away.

Without it she felt adrift and uncertain, and, over the next week, behaved in a compliant if rather distant manner. When Whit insisted on driving her to Boston for her hospital appointment, she acquiesced.

Kip assumed that once she was admitted and installed in a wheelchair he would leave. When he showed no sign of it she said, 'Thanks for bringing me, but I wouldn't bother hanging around. I'll probably be here for hours.'

'I have to stay…isn't that right, Nurse?' he appealed to the middle-aged woman who had just taken her details.

'Of course,' the nurse confirmed, returning his conspiratorial smile.

Kip wondered if any woman was immune to his charm. 'Look, I'll be fine,' she assured him heavily. 'If they're keeping me in for… Well, if there's a problem—' the word 'amputation' stuck in her throat '—they could phone you at college.'

'I've already taken the day off,' he informed her, clearly intent on remaining.

But Kip didn't want it. She felt that she could cope with bad news if she was alone. With him there she might just break down.

'Listen, I don't need you here,' she finally said, more bluntly than she'd intended.

It shocked the nurse, who glanced at her as if questioning her sanity.

Kip regretted the words too as Whit's brow creased for a moment before he said, 'I can't argue with that.'

He turned on his heel and walked away.

Kip stared after him in confusion. Had she hurt him? No, she couldn't have. Whit Delaney was too strong to let such a small thing bother him.

She saw condemnation in the nurse's eyes and found herself on the defensive. 'I suppose you think I'm horrible too.'

'Not my place to think one way or the other, child,' the woman drawled in a distinctive Southern accent, 'but I sure wouldn't let that one get away if he were mine.'

'Well, he isn't!' Kip denied adamantly, then thought to add, 'Mine either, I mean… He's just…' She trailed off, unable to explain what Whit Delaney was to her. She didn't know herself. 'No one,' she finally concluded, denying any real relationship.

The nurse looked sceptical but confined herself to muttering, 'Wish I knew a no one like that,' as she wheeled Kip along a corridor.

Kip remained silent this time, but felt guilty long afterwards. What was wrong with her? Why did she keep throwing Whit's kindness back in his face? She asked herself the question but avoided searching too hard for the answer. She promised herself instead that, no matter what happened, she would learn some gratitude.

It was a gruelling morning as first her cast was removed then a series of tests and X-rays were performed on her leg and ankle. Finally she was wheeled to a private room, and she expected the worst. It was noon before the surgeon arrived to deliver his verdict.

She was crying hard when Whit appeared soon afterwards. She tried to stop but it was as if a dam had burst. He sat on the bed and put his arms out to her. She tried to pull away but he held onto her and, too weak to struggle, she collapsed into his arms.

He let her cry herself out before he spoke. 'I'm so goddamn sorry, kid.'

Kip shook her head against his shoulder. 'You don't understand. I'm not going to lose my foot.'

'I know. The doctor told me.' He cradled her head to his chest. 'But he told me the rest too.'

The surgeon hadn't been certain. He had spoken in probabilities, like a betting man. The odds were long against her ever running competitively again.

Kip shook her head again and took a hard swallow, trying to find the words to explain. She wasn't crying because her athletics career was over. She was crying with sheer relief that she would at least walk again. Perhaps her obsession had died in the accident or just faded away in the time since, but right at that moment she didn't care if she never ran again.

'It's not the end of the world, Kip,' he continued gently. 'You're bright enough to do anything you want to.'

'No, you don't understand.' Kip tried to say that it was all right. 'It was just that I was so scared before...' she choked out, admitting her true feelings for once.

'I know. I know,' he repeated, trying to soothe her, to take away the pain that he imagined she still felt.

He went on holding her, and for once Kip allowed herself the luxury of being close to another human being. Long after she stopped crying she remained in his arms, drawing from his strength and warmth.

They were finally interrupted by the entrance of a nurse. Kip lifted her head away from Whit's shoulder in time to catch a look of satisfaction on the other woman's face. It wasn't hard to read; it was the same nurse who had admitted her.

'Ready to go home?' Whit asked her simply, and Kip nodded without thinking.

It was only later, when they drove from Boston to Radford and the day turned to dusk, that she realised that that was how it felt. She was going home.

What might have been—the loss of her foot—helped Kip bear what followed. Her plaster cast might have been off, but there were no instant miracles on offer.

For the first three weeks each step was agony. A taxi took
her to a physiotherapy clinic where she was put through an
exercise programme that came close to torture at times. But
Kip was stoical and uncomplaining, and driven with a new
goal in mind—to walk without a limp.

On the second weekend Whit drove her to the clinic and
hung round the gym while she went through her treatment.
Tears no longer collected in her eyes when she used her leg,
but the lines of pain were clearly etched on her face.

At the end of the session Whit asked the therapist straight,
'Do you have to be quite so tough on her?'

'No,' the man replied, 'but you try slowing her down.' He
slid Kip a wry look before saying, 'Got to go. See you tomorrow, Kip.'

'See you, Matt.' Kip directed a brief smile at the big, burly
therapist.

Whit realised what the man meant and asked her, 'So why
the hurry?'

Kip didn't answer.

He answered for her. 'Still chasing that gold.'

'No,' Kip denied adamantly, 'it's not that. It's just—I want
to be independent again. I've already stayed too long at your
father's.'

'Who says?' It was a rhetorical question, it seemed, for he
ran on, 'Not my father, that's for sure. He thinks, and I quote,
you're "a darling of a girl".'

'Me?' Kip's face mirrored disbelief.

'Yes, even allowing for my father's Irish ancestry, the de-
scription took me by surprise too,' he agreed drily, 'but no
more than Mrs Novak's. She refers to you as "that sweet
child".'

Kip's eyes rounded, then narrowed on him. 'You're making that up.'

'As God is my witness, I'm not.' He held up a hand to
swear to it. 'And that only leaves Abby, whose devotion
cannot be disputed.'

Kip didn't know what to say. All these weeks she'd imagined that the adult occupants of 10 Washington Avenue were

tolerating her out of kindness and quietly counting the days to her departure, but Whit was suggesting something quite different.

'And you?' Kip realised he'd left himself out of the equation.

'Me?' He caught her eyes for a moment and she saw her own reservations reflected back at her. 'Oh, I'm sure I can put up with you for a few more months.'

'Thanks.' Kip pulled a face, but without any real animosity.

She was no longer sure what she felt for Whit. From their very first meeting she had resented him—his intelligence, his confidence, his sheer masculinity. She had wanted to hate him and he'd given her a reason that night in her apartment. Not because he'd taken her virginity; even in her darkest moods she had never seen herself as a helpless victim. It was for touching her, reaching her, destroying her immunity to life.

Till then she had existed in a world of her own making— a sterile place where she felt almost nothing. He had drawn her from the shadows into a world which, at first, had promised only pain. For that she had hated him.

But it had grown hard to sustain such an emotion, or justify it, when Whit had taken care of her in a way no one else ever had. No matter if he did it out of guilt or pity. Another man might have walked away. Kip saw that now.

'Anyway, you've got to stay,' he went on, smiling, 'and save Abby from my sorrowful choice in babysitters.'

'Anyone might have been taken in by Stacey,' Kip remarked generously.

'Possibly,' he conceded, 'but she was one in a legion of babysitters, housekeepers and women in general that prove I have disastrous judgement in that area.'

Surprised by his honesty, Kip muttered an inadequate 'Oh.'

Later, in the car, she wondered if she was included in the 'women in general'—or had that been an oblique reference to his wife? He never talked of her, perhaps because it was still a painful subject. But Mrs Novak had no such reticence and had already relayed the whole story to Kip.

Apparently Whit had met, courted, married, had a baby by and been divorced from his actress wife all in the space of two and a half years. According to Mrs Novak, Elizabeth Carlton had been a vain, selfish, silly young woman who had put her career before her husband and child and had abandoned both when they proved too much trouble.

When she'd eventually reclaimed Abby, it had been the ultimate act of selfishness, treating her daughter as an accessory when motherhood suddenly became fashionable in Hollywood. Whereas if Whit was guilty of anything it was of being a romantic; anyone else with half an eye open would have seen that the English girl's charm was skin-deep.

Kip didn't know how much of this was bias on the housekeeper's part, but Abby was clearly less grieved by her mother's death than relieved to be back living with her father.

Kip didn't blame the child. As a father, Whit Delaney was brilliant—strong when he needed to be, but gentle and patient too. He listened to his daughter, made her laugh, loved her uncritically.

Kip watched them together and realised just how far short her own father had fallen of the parental ideal. Such realisation could have made Kip bitter but it actually had the opposite effect. She seemed to be losing some of her cynicism and wariness in the Delaney household.

Weeks slipped into months as her life became a busy round of physiotherapy, studying and childminding. After Easter she returned to her computer classes at college, although she didn't expect to pass any exams.

She remained with the older professor for her literature studies, and in June sat the same papers as the other students. By that time she was walking without difficulty, well ahead of any predictions, and had started looking for a summer job, intending to go back to college in the fall. Though she had lost her athletics scholarship, Radford had offered her another as a foreign-exchange student.

'I hear you're looking for a summer job,' Whit said one afternoon when they passed in the hall. 'Anything specific?'

'I may have found one—waiting tables at Charlie's Diner,' she replied in a tone that dared him to comment. She knew that it was a rough sort of place.

He confined himself to a brief 'Should you be using your leg that much?'

'I'm fine,' Kip dismissed. 'Matt said so.'

'Not quite.' Whit had talked to her therapist too. 'He says there's still a weakness in the ankle and you should take it easy if you want it to mend one hundred per cent.'

Kip knew all this. 'I have to get a job,' she told him.

'And jeopardise any chance of returning to full fitness?' He pointed out the possible cost, then added, 'Anyway, you already have a job—looking after Abby.'

'Not for very much longer,' Kip commented tightly. 'I understand you're going back to Maine when she gets her vacation.'

He hadn't told her. She'd learned it from Alice Novak, who functioned as a bulletin board in the house. She'd known that it was coming but she'd still felt distraught. She'd put that down to losing Abby, and coped with it by planning her own future.

'Yes, I've been meaning to have a talk with you,' he went on. 'Abby'll need the summer to settle back there before school recommences in the fall... I was hoping you'd come with us.' He caught her eyes and she made the mistake of looking straight back at him.

For a moment Kip's heart hammered hard against her rib-cage as he gave her a look of seeming tenderness.

Then he continued quietly, 'It would really help Abby. It's almost a year since we lived there and it'll take her a while to make friends again.'

Kip came back to earth with a bump. He wanted her for Abby's sake. What else?

'I'd pay you, of course,' he added, in the face of her lengthening silence.

'Of course,' Kip echoed a little harshly.

'That wasn't meant as an insult.' He caught her tone, if not the reason behind it. 'I wouldn't want financial considerations to stop you coming with us.'

'I…' Kip told herself to say no, but it came out as a very uncertain 'I don't know.'

Whit sensed indecision and took advantage. 'It could benefit both of us. We live a very simple life in Maine; you'll have a chance to take it easy and get fit at the same time. I'll have someone to look after Abby and possibly manage to finish the novel I promised my publisher last March.'

He made it sound a mutually favourable business arrangement. Kip was still tempted, but then he'd caught her at a vulnerable moment. She'd spent the morning job-hunting and had forgotten what things were like in the real world. Six months with the Delaneys had turned her soft. Did she want to spend her days and nights waiting on rude, roughneck characters who believed that waitresses actually liked getting their bottoms pinched?

'Well, think about it.' He shrugged at her hesitation.

'I've thought about it,' Kip replied quickly. 'I'll come to Maine.'

He looked surprised by her sudden decision, then positively triumphant. A wide, slanting smile spread across his face and reminded her that he was the best-looking man she'd ever met. It seemed that she was never going to get used to that fact.

'To babysit for Abby,' she added for her own benefit.

But he was well ahead of her. 'Of course. What else? I made a promise, remember?'

A promise he had rigorously adhered to. He hadn't kissed her and had barely touched her since that New Year's night. Whatever attraction she'd held for him seemed to have died then.

'At any rate, I've always found coming on to women profoundly difficult with an eight-year-old in the house,' he added, laughing at any lingering doubts she might have had.

Kip felt her cheeks betray her with a blush, but her voice was cool enough. 'I'm really not worried about that.'

'Good. Then that's settled,' he announced before she had a change of mind. 'A week Friday.'

'A week Friday', Kip repeated to herself as he disappeared through to the study and left her wondering what she'd committed herself to.

It turned out, in fact, to be the best time of her life. Maine was heaven on earth, and so was his house. It sat on a stretch of Atlantic coastline, and though not big by some standards it still took her breath away with its walls of glass and wide, open terraces overlooking the sea.

There was only one floor of living accommodation but a section of it was designed as guest quarters and Kip had these, ensuring her some privacy. Not that she spent much time there.

They quickly fell into a routine. Mornings Abby and she would go beachcombing or swimming, or catch the bus into the nearest town and go to the local ice-cream parlour. Midday Whit would emerge, having worked till the small hours and slept late. Often he would do the cooking, because Kip had only a limited range of dishes, taught her by Mrs Novak. Then they would go out together, sailing or water-skiing, or just into town for groceries.

It wasn't a big place, although its population was increased in the summer months by tourists. It seemed, despite his absence, that the townspeople accepted Whit as one of their own.

What they made of Kip's place in the scheme of things was harder to tell. Whit didn't introduce her as an employee, just as his friend—a relationship open to all kinds of interpretation. It was Kip who insisted on advertising her identity as nanny. However, it drew more speculative looks and wry smiles than Whit's vaguer claim, and after a while Kip learned to keep quiet.

That summer Kip fell in love. Not with the man—she told herself—but with his house and his way of life and the sounds and sight and smell of an ocean. That summer she looked no further than the next day and learned how to be happy. She wanted it to last for ever, but nothing did.

It came almost as a shock when Abby finally restarted school. Kip was due back in college a month later; by some miracle she'd done well enough in her term papers to enter her second year.

Whit asked her to hang around for Abby's first couple of weeks in school, and Kip didn't need much persuading. Even with Abby at school there was enough to do round the house to justify the wage Whit paid her, and in the spare time she had she started running again.

It wasn't part of some grand plan. She no longer thought in terms of races or medals. She just felt unfit after a summer of indulgence and, with the blessing of a physiotherapist, decided to run for exercise. Whit didn't say anything but he looked disappointed.

Kip tried to explain that she was merely running for pleasure but he clearly didn't believe her, and she got cross with herself for even bothering to justify her actions. He paid her wage; he didn't own her. Soon she would be gone—out of his life and Abby's.

As the day came closer Kip's spirits sank lower and lower. She was just scared, she told herself. She had grown too used to having people round her. She had to learn to be on her own again. In this world she could only really count on herself.

She began to separate herself from the Delaneys. In the evenings, when she usually sat with them, she went out running instead. It fuelled Whit's suspicions that she was becoming obsessed again, but Kip didn't care. She had to get a life for herself. She had to get out of theirs.

She returned one night, jogging along the hard sand at the water's edge, and found him sitting on the terrace. He called out to her when she would have disappeared inside.

'I wanted to talk to you but you'd disappeared,' he said as she climbed up the steps from the beach.

Kip took it as criticism and defended herself. 'I finished the washing-up first.'

He raised an exasperated brow. 'Do you think I give a damn about washing-up, Kip? Come on, sit down and don't go all Mrs Novak on me.'

Kip remained standing and bristled back, 'I don't know what you mean.'

'Yes, you do,' he countered. 'You're not here as my housekeeper, which is just as well, because between your limited culinary skills and your haphazard cleaning techniques I would have fired you by now.'

'Well, don't let me stop you!' Kip was stung by his comments—true though they were.

He didn't retaliate immediately but gave her a long, hard look. 'Are you really that anxious to get back to Radford?'

It was a serious question—so serious that Kip couldn't bring herself to give a flippant answer—or any answer at all.

He rose from the table where he'd been sitting and came round to stand before her. 'Because if you're not,' he went on, his voice deep and steady, 'I'd really like you to stay.'

'Stay?' Kip echoed, her mouth dry. 'For how long?'

'I don't know.' His face remained straight and unsmiling. 'A month, a year, a lifetime? Who knows how long?'

What was he asking? His eyes gave her the answer but Kip blinded herself to it.

'You want me to stay for Abby,' she concluded.

He shook his head and said without ambiguity, 'I want you to stay for me.'

'I d-don't—'

'Understand? It's simple enough. Do you really want me to explain it?'

'I... N-no.' Kip could read the reason quite clearly in his eyes; how had she missed the desire in them all these months? 'But you haven't...'

'Touched you.' He finished her sentence for her again. 'I made a promise... If you stay, I shall need to be released from that promise.'

'I—I...' Kip opened her mouth but no protest came out. She was paralysed by his directness.

He had it all worked out. 'You don't have to abandon college. You can transfer to a similar course at Augusta. I've checked.'

Kip stared at him speechlessly. How long had he been thinking about this, planning it?

'We'd have to explain things to Abby, of course,' Whit continued, encouraged by the fact that she hadn't slapped his face yet. 'I don't anticipate any objection, but clarification of the situation would be quite important.'

He sounded so clinical that Kip's surprise gave way to a cold pride. 'Perhaps you'd like to clarify it for me first?'

Whit grimaced. 'I'm sorry. I expressed myself badly. I just meant that Abby might think our living together was a prelude to marriage, and it wouldn't be right to get her hopes up.'

Or anyone else's for that matter, Kip assumed, receiving the message loud and clear.

She turned his words back on him. 'No, you're right. I would never marry you.'

'No, I meant—' He broke off as he realised she'd known exactly what he meant. 'I guess I deserved that... As you say, why should you want to marry me?'

'Unless it was for your money,' Kip suggested, over the first shock and fighting back.

But her frankness just made him laugh. 'Yes, I suppose that is one of my more attractive qualities.'

He went on smiling at her and Kip, a traitor to herself, smiled back. Why, she didn't know. This man had just propositioned her. Where was her outrage?

'Anyway, think about it,' he added, as if it were a casual matter.

Perhaps it was to him. Kip wondered if he'd lived with other women before Abby had come back into his life.

'I—I...' She caught his arm when he would have gone inside.

'Yes?' He turned expectantly.

'I...' Kip shook her head. 'This is absurd.'

He raised a questioning brow. 'Which? My asking you this way or my asking at all?'

'I don't know,' she replied, still shaking her head. 'Both, I suppose.'

'Would it help if I kissed you?'

'Kissed me?'

'It might demonstrate my feelings for you.' He caught and held her eyes.

That look alone made Kip's head swim; when he lifted a hand to smooth back her hair, her heart was in her mouth.

'Please, don't!' she said in an unsteady voice.

'You don't mean that.' His palm caressed the softness of her cheek.

He was right. She wanted him to kiss her. She wanted it so badly that it frightened her.

'Come live with me.' He pressed his lips to her forehead.

She started to tremble. She was already lost, even before he'd touched her. She shook her head, denying her own feelings.

It was a small gesture but it saved her. Bound by his promise, Whit ignored his body's urges and set her from him. 'OK. Think about it.'

'I—I...' Kip felt a longing as sharp as a knife in her side and almost ran back into his arms.

Whit read the desire in her eyes. He wasn't blind. But he didn't just want one night when her resistance was lowered. 'You'd better go in now.'

His voice had hardened and brought Kip back to reality. What was she doing, even listening to this?

She ran from him then, but couldn't run from the feelings he'd reawakened. She told herself that it *was* absurd. She and Whit Delaney. He was too smart, too rich, too mature—too everything to be interested in a nobody like her. She told herself that it wasn't Whitman Delaney she loved but the house, and Abby, and being inside a family for the first time

in her life. She told herself that it would end in grief, and
that grief would be hers.

But no amount of common sense changed her feelings. She
wanted to stay more than she'd ever wanted anything else in
her life.

CHAPTER NINE

EVENTS moved quickly the next day. As it was a Saturday, Abby was around, and so conversation was impossible. It was lunchtime before Whit announced, 'My father's driving up this afternoon.'

'Great. I can show Gramps my shell collection,' Abby said happily, without noticing that the statement had been directed at Kip.

'He thought you might need a lift down to Radford.' Blue eyes rested on Kip, questioning her intention.

Would she return with his father or stay?

'But Kip's not going back till next week,' Abby protested.

'Your grandfather can't come then,' he replied, to the child this time, 'and he feels Kip should go back to Radford sooner rather than later.'

'Why?' Abby was puzzled.

He gave some general answer, about textbooks to be bought, but Kip realised that it wasn't the true reason.

'You've told your father,' she concluded in disbelief.

He nodded. 'My wishes, yes. Yours, I couldn't vouch for.'

'Told him what?' Abby looked from one adult face to the other. 'What are you two talking about?'

'I'll explain later, perhaps,' her father replied briefly.

'Typical.' Abby gave a loud sigh. 'You'll explain when I get older, right?'

'Maybe sooner.' He caught Kip's eye once more.

'Well, I sure won't hold my breath,' Abby muttered, and, deciding that they were both acting strange, the way adults sometimes did, excused herself from the lunch table.

'Have you decided?' Whit asked Kip the moment the child disappeared.

Kip ignored the question and asked one of her own. 'Why did you tell your father?'

'I didn't directly,' he stated. 'I mentioned you might be staying on and he guessed the rest... That's why he's hot-footing it up here. To talk you out of it.'

'Or you,' she countered. After all, Alex Delaney was *his* father.

He shook his head. 'My father feels I can take the pain. It's you he's concerned for.'

'Will there be pain?' Kip's question was no more crazy than the whole conversation.

Whit might have lied, but not to this girl. 'Possibly. But I'd never hurt you deliberately.' He looked at her with a tenderness that suggested that hurting her was the last thing he'd do. 'I can't promise happy-ever-afters, Kip. I'm too old or too cynical to believe in them any more. But I do care for you. And I need you...I certainly want you.' His mouth twisted, admitting his desire and frustration. 'Stay and live with me, Kip?'

Every scrap of sense and reason screamed no, but Kip wasn't listening. She was in some dream world, drawn there by his eyes—eyes that spoke of feelings more eloquently than his words.

Her lips formed an answer, might have even said it aloud. She remembered him smiling fleetingly before Abby descended on them once more.

They never got a chance to discuss the matter. It was probably as well, for Abby's interruption was closely followed by his father's appearance—and everything changed after that.

Alex Delaney bided his time, playing with his granddaughter a while before seeking out Kip in the kitchen. She was preparing the evening meal and seemed very much at home.

'You look well,' he remarked as she glanced up and caught him watching her.

'Thanks.' Kip smiled back. 'The doctor thinks my leg has mended completely.'

'That's good.' Alex Delaney nodded in satisfaction. 'Perhaps you'll be able to pick up your athletics career.'

'Perhaps.' Kip had no such ambition, but it was easier to agree.

Alex Delaney pursued the subject. 'Whit tells me you're running again. Bill Scott will be pleased to hear it. According to Bill, you were the most natural athlete he'd ever trained.'

'I don't know if I want to go back to running,' Kip finally admitted. 'Not on a serious level.'

'Yes, well…Whit's suggested you and he may have other plans.' The professor at last got to the point.

'Yes,' Kip answered briefly, and avoided his eye as she prepared a salad.

'Look, I know it's not my business and you may call me an interfering old man…' He paused as if he expected her to do just that.

Kip remained silent, too fond of him to be rude and too embarrassed to defend herself.

'But have you really thought this through?' He chose his words carefully.

'You don't think we're suited,' Kip concluded for him.

'No…at least, I don't know.' Alex was caught with his feet in two camps. 'Whit believes you are.'

Kip hid her surprise. 'What has he said?'

'That you never bore him, never nag him and never intrude in his space…whatever that means.'

It was hardly the most romantic of outlooks. Even Kip conceded that. But neither of them had talked of love or lifelong commitment.

It was Alex Delaney who felt that that was lacking. 'Kipling, at the risk of being disloyal to my son, I have to warn you—I don't think your relationship with him will prove a lasting one.'

'It's all right, Professor,' Kip assured him with a brief smile, 'your son's already issued the same warning. I won't be suing him for breach of promise.'

'Then why...?' Alex Delaney hesitated to ask why she should accept so little commitment.

Kip wondered too. Perhaps Whit wasn't the only one it suited. She had spent her life moving from one place to another. Could she ever really settle down?

'Do you love my son?' he added very quietly.

Kip's heart beat hard against her ribs. It always did when she thought of Whit in that way. But she still distrusted and discounted emotion.

'I don't think I know how to love,' she stated in reply.

Alex Delaney's eyes shaded with sadness rather than disapproval. Whit had told him much of her background. It was why he felt that he had to protect her, over and above his son's happiness.

'Then is it gratitude?' He resumed his questioning.

Kip frowned, unsure of what he meant.

'Because if it is,' he went on, 'then it's misguided. My son paid your hospital bills expecting nothing in return. He would be the first to tell you that. And, though the amount might seem large to you, it's a drop in the ocean to him.'

'He paid my bills?' Kip repeated in total shock.

Alex Delaney quickly realised his mistake. 'I thought you knew.'

'All my bills?' she demanded in a harsh whisper.

He nodded and watched with concern the emotions working across Kip's face.

Shock gave way to anger, at Whit and at her own stupidity. Suddenly other things made sense. The doctor had talked of her benefactor and she'd assumed that he'd meant the college. The same doctor had allowed Whit into one consultation without explanation, and had, in retrospect, clearly been deferring to him as his client. Why had she not seen it at the time?

'Kipling—' Alex Delaney caught her arm when she looked ready to go somewhere and explode '—I shouldn't have told you. It clearly isn't relevant to the current situation.'

'Isn't it?'

'Well, no—if you didn't know, then you're hardly confusing gratitude with whatever you do feel for my son.'

'You're right. I'm not grateful.' She was furious and humiliated. Why had no one told her—or asked her, for that matter? She would never have taken his charity.

'I can see I've made you angry.' Alex Delaney was now wishing that he hadn't interfered in a relationship that was proving more complicated than he'd imagined. 'Please, don't do anything until you've calmed down.'

'I am calm.' Kip was suddenly deadly calm. She'd emerged from a dream into the harsh light of reality. Had she actually imagined that she could ever have a relationship with Whit Delaney in which she would in any way be his equal? If she had, then owing him for hundreds of thousands of dollars' worth of medical treatment was surely disillusionment. 'Professor, will you drive me back to Radford?'

'Tomorrow, you mean?'

'No, now.'

'I—I…' Though it was what he'd intended when he'd come up here, Alex Delaney was no longer sure if he'd done the right thing. 'If you want,' he agreed reluctantly.

'I'll go pack my bag.'

Kip's anger carried her down the corridor, past the living room. She didn't seek out Whit. She would explode if she did, and Abby might be hit by the fall-out.

She threw clothes and books and photographs and shells and mementoes in a jumble into her case. The photographs spilled out of their folder; the top one was of her and Abby, smiling into the camera, taken by Whit. She collected them together and tossed them back out of the case. She threw out the shells next, and anything else that she'd acquired in Maine. She would travel light as she always did. No room for sentiment.

'Kip?' He stood framed in the doorway, watching.

She didn't turn, didn't stop, zipped up her case and lifted it off the bed. 'Your father's taking me back to Radford,' she stated, crossing towards the door.

She was too angry to look at him. She stared at a point

past his shoulder and waited for him to get out of her way. He didn't move.

'Not this moment he's not,' he told her. 'He's just taken Abby for a meal in town.'

Kip's gaze switched to him, her eyes betraying both anger and hurt. In the end his father had deserted her. But what had she expected? She was the outsider.

'I'll catch a bus. Please get out of my way,' she instructed him tightly.

'You can't leave like this.' He took a step towards her.

Kip backed away. She mustn't let him touch her.

He saw the panic on her face but read it as temper. 'OK, you're mad because I didn't tell you about your hospital bills. Maybe you have a right to be. I don't know. But it's not such a big deal—'

'You lied!' she accused him in bitter tones. 'You said I was covered by college insurance.'

'And the truth would have been preferable?' he threw back. 'You were lying in hospital, recovering from an accident, hating the world in general and me in particular. I'm sure you'd have loved to hear you were beholden to me in any way.'

The word 'beholden' was anathema to Kip's pride. 'So when were you saving it for? Now, maybe? An inducement to shack up with you?'

Till that point Whit had been going easy with her, but she'd just stepped over the mark.

'I've never paid for sex in my life,' he bit back, 'but if I was going to I could sure get someone a whole lot more experienced for hundreds of thousands of dollars.'

The insult stung; the sum sent her reeling. *How much?*

Even as she spat out the words, 'I'll pay it back,' she knew that she was being ridiculous. How could she ever hope to?

'I don't want it,' he said dismissively. 'That's not the point. What's between you and me is wholly separate from your medical bill. I didn't pay it to buy you.'

'Why did you, then?' she demanded.

'Who knows?' He shrugged, then admitted, 'Guilt, I guess.

An hour after we have a fairly heavy conversation you're stepping out in front of cars.'

'It wasn't deliberate!'

'I'm not saying it was. I just felt there might be some connection.'

Kip supposed that there had been. She'd done the pregnancy test, then left the store in a daze.

'Anyway, my father was talking of putting his life savings on the line for you,' he ran on, 'so I had little choice... But it doesn't matter. I'm not going to miss the money,' he assured her, shrugging off an amount that had sounded like a fortune to Kip.

'I'll pay it back,' she repeated, although right at that moment she hadn't the faintest idea how.

'To hell with the money!' Whit struggled to contain anger and exasperation. 'Why should it change anything? You already agreed to stay.'

Perhaps Kip had this morning, but it now seemed like madness. Had she really thought that she could be happy in so unequal a relationship? She had no money—other than what he gave her. No home outside this. No future without being his mistress.

She shook her head and kept on shaking it as she realised how things would be. 'I've changed my mind.'

The hardness in her eyes told Whit that she meant it. He saw that it was over—over before it had ever really begun.

'I wonder if you know what you're doing to me, Kipling Wilson?' he said in low, unsteady tones.

Kip heard the emotion in his voice but put it down to anger and frustration. That's all.

'Chalk it up to experience, Professor,' she retaliated. 'No one ever has a perfect track record.'

Whit didn't understand the comment, but he saw what was happening. It was as if the months they'd been together had never been. He was looking at the same girl he had first met—tough and insular and closed to any real emotion. Had he been fooling himself all this time?

Kip registered the disillusionment in his stare but it made

her angrier. 'I'm sure there are plenty of other little girl students you can seduce,' she continued harshly, 'from the local college campus.'

It was hitting below the belt. Kip realised it even before his face went rigid. He took another step towards her, and left the doorway clear. She picked up her bag and tried to make her getaway.

'Uh-uh.' He grabbed her arm and the suitcase fell from her other. 'You don't say something like that and just walk away.'

'Let me go!' Kip masked shame with indignation.

'Not till we get a few things straight.' He held her there, fingers locked round her wrist. 'Like the fact you were it— the only student I've ever talked into bed. And, from memory, you sure didn't need a lot of persuading.'

'You bastard!' Kip lifted her other hand to push him or slap him or something. He caught her arm mid-flight.

'You started this game of truth,' he bit out, 'so let's finish it.'

'If you don't let me go,' Kip began to threaten him, 'I'll— '

'You'll…?' He raised a taunting brow, believing that there was nothing she could do.

He was wrong. She kicked him. She did it without thinking, and couldn't believe she'd done it, afterwards.

A stupid thing to do. It didn't gain her freedom. It just threw out the rules.

He pushed her hard against the door and effectively trapped her there with his body.

'Kick me again,' he growled, 'and I'll kick you back.'

'I—I…' Kip looked up into his face and any words of defiance dried up.

His eyes were dark with temper, his jaw rigid. She had never seen him like this. She stopped struggling and went still.

'That's better,' he said, but his voice was low and dangerous as he ran on, 'So let's see how much persuading you need these days.'

His eyes told her what he intended. She tried to look away, but he caught her chin and forced her to meet his gaze.

She shook her head in wordless protest. It didn't stop him. He touched her lips with his finger. Her breath quickened. She tried to hold it rather than betray herself. But he already knew. He could probably hear her heart hammering against her ribs.

He held her head as he slowly lowered his, still watching with those compelling blue eyes. Her lips were parted before his mouth even touched hers. Her heart turned over and she felt such a rush of emotion that it was frightening.

He was right. She needed no persuading. Nothing else felt like this. His lips moved over hers, breathing life into her; his body enfolded hers, making it fluid. She had been born for this.

Whit felt her tremble as he started to touch her, to run his hands over her body, pulling at her clothes. He wanted to touch all of her. His mouth left hers as he turned her in his arms and drew her towards the bed.

Some vestige of sanity returned to Kip as he pulled her down with him onto the counterpane. She asked herself what she was doing. What was she letting him do? But still she didn't stop him.

He unbuttoned her shirt and drew apart the sides. He found her naked beneath. She looked at him, but he wasn't looking at her. His eyes were following his hand, sliding up over her ribcage to the soft, full flesh he'd exposed.

Kip's lips formed the word 'no', but it was lost in a gasp as he leaned forward and put his mouth to her breast. It was both shock and delight: his tongue slowly licking, his teeth gently biting, five o'clock shadow rough and unfamiliar against her soft skin. Breathing became difficult, thinking impossible as he sucked and played on her swollen nipple.

Blindly, instinctively, she sought his hand and lifted it to her other breast, needing him to touch, caress, satisfy the ache that spread through her body.

She was shaking when he finally lifted his mouth to hers once more. She held onto his neck, his hair, kissing him, wanting him, wanting it all. He dragged off his own shirt, not caring that he ripped it, then pulled her close.

Desire was a living thing, twisting through her body like a snake. Desire was a drug, heady and illicit, making her senses swim. Desire was a weakness that was destroying her.

'No!' This time she cried out the word—a high, panicked sound.

She pushed at his shoulders and he realised what was happening. He released her and sat up, away from her.

Whit was more frustrated than angry. He stared down at her in the failing light. She looked confused, haunted, with the eyes of a child. Her face had acquired beauty over the summer. Her body was less like a boy's. He could see her perfect white breasts through her open shirt and he wanted to touch her again.

'I won't hurt you,' he promised softly.

She shook her head. He didn't understand. But she did. If they did this, she would be his. Not for a day or a week or a year—his for ever. But he didn't want that. He had said so.

He stretched out and touched her face with the back of his hand. She flinched and rolled away, sitting up at the far edge of the bed. She rebuttoned her blouse with clumsy fingers and hastily tucked it in her trousers before standing.

He stood too, saying when she turned, 'I'm sorry. I didn't mean to rush you. I can wait.'

'It's no big deal. You were just making your point,' she responded bitterly.

'My point?' Whit had forgotten what had led them there.

Kip hadn't. 'It seems I'm easy, like you said.'

'*Easy?*' he repeated, and gave a brief laugh. 'That certainly isn't a word I'd use. Frustrating, maybe. Maddening, definitely. Volatile and a few other things—but never easy.' He shook his head, then gave her a slow smile, suggesting that he liked her the way she was.

But before Kip could think through her own feelings for him she heard a car door slamming outside.

'That'll be my father and Abby.'

'Good.'

Kip smoothed her hair down and crossed to pick up her case from the floor where it had fallen.

He watched in disbelief. 'You're still going?'

She nodded and walked to the door. She was out in the corridor before he could stop her.

Alex Delaney met her in the hall. He saw her case and gave a silent nod of understanding.

Abby was slower to catch on. When she did, she started to cry a little.

Kip wanted to cry too, but not then. She put on a brave face for Abby and returned the girl's fierce hug with a promise to write.

She didn't turn round, didn't see the expression on Whit's face. If she had, she would have realised that she wasn't the only one hurting.

Alex Delaney saw it and wished that he'd never interfered. He had done so for the best of motives but it was hard to be sure he'd been right. It got harder as he drove back to Radford with a girl whose eyes seemed utterly dead of emotion.

Only Kip knew her terrible secret. She had discovered it that afternoon when she lay in Whit Delaney's arms, his mouth covering hers, his hands on her skin, his body hard against hers. She had wanted to lie down with him and make love once more.

She had finally understood. Love wasn't just a four-letter word. It wasn't the imaginary thing she'd always believed it to be. Love was pain and longing, terrifying in its power.

And love was what she'd run from that afternoon, before it destroyed her for ever.

CHAPTER TEN

Kip warmed up at the side of the track with the other runners. The venue was the Los Angeles stadium, built for the 1984 Olympics. The race was five thousand metres. The field was international. The date was the fifteenth of August.

A whole year had gone by and much had happened to Kip. She'd returned to Radford with the professor and, at his insistence, stayed at Washington Avenue, repaying her living expenses with some cooking and cleaning. She had gone back to college, and within three months had made it back on the athletics team. By Easter she had been running better than she had ever done before, and had clocked a time that put her in the world's top thirty.

After that things had moved rapidly. A man called Ben Shaw had invited her to train at his athletics camp in Nevada; in return he got a percentage of all purses, advertising fees and sponsorship deals she might make in the future.

Of course it was no longer athletics. Money was the real name of the game. Ben Shaw hoped that he could turn her into a million-dollar billboard. And who was she to argue? Money kept Kip focused too.

She took up her starting position on the track. She didn't look up at the crowd; she'd made that mistake in the heats and had lost concentration. She had just scraped through to the finals. She needed to be in the first three to clinch a deal with a sportswear giant. She also needed it for herself—to be a success in her own right, not someone's charity case or pet project.

There was a delay in the race start. By the time the gun went Kip was like a highly strung racehorse, desperate to escape from the starting gate. She got away fast and was fifth or sixth in the first group of runners. However, they soon settled down to a pace too slow for record times. An unrated Dutch girl made an early break but Kip resisted following her. Instead she kept within striking distance of the Rumanian who was expected to win and a Swedish runner, also ranked in the world's top ten.

Neither saw Kip as a danger. She was barely known, and, after a disappointing heat, largely discounted. When the last lap bell sounded there was the usual tussle for position. This was where Kip had often lost out in the past, but she had acquired a new ruthlessness since her accident.

She saw a gap and charged through it like a steeplechaser, just missing being spiked by another runner. The move put her in fourth position, but already the first two had broken away from the bunch. She overtook the third girl by going wide on a bend, then had to increase her pace to close the gap and stay in contention. It was just her, the Swede and the Rumanian for the last five hundred metres, but the other two were running their own private race, anticipating no real competition from the rest of the field.

With three hundred metres left the others kicked up a gear, but so did Kip, remaining tucked behind. The other two were still discounting her as they vied for first and second. Neither appreciated that Kip had a sprint finish. She saved it till the final bend and at first it seemed that she'd left it too late. A hundred metres to the tape and the others were neck and neck, with Kip a couple of strides behind, but she was gaining, and she suddenly knew that she could do it.

She kicked again and drew level. It took the Swedish girl by surprise and she seemed to fade. There was just the Rumanian to beat and, at thirty metres, there was nothing in it. They took it to the line, touching the tape at virtually the same split second.

A roar went up from the crowd, applauding a race that had been a battle to the finish. Kip ran off the track and half folded over, lungs tearing at her, muscles hurting; she actually had to concentrate on not being physically sick. She wasn't aware that she'd won till the Rumanian came and clapped her on the back. Even then she wasn't sure if it was consolation for coming second. It wasn't until her trainer appeared to shout out at her, 'You did it! You did it!' that she realised.

She had won. Despite a world-class field, she, Kipling Wilson, had won. And, in that first moment, it was only the running that mattered, and her face was a beaming reflection of her pride in it.

Then the media descended, microphones extended, jostling for position to talk to the latest running sensation. They asked how she felt and when she answered, 'Breathless,' they laughed, although she hadn't intentionally been making a joke. They asked about her background and she gave vague and guarded answers about coming to America on a college scholarship. One started to ask about her personal life and Kip suddenly understood that she'd become public property.

She managed to escape then, but it was a temporary reprieve. By the time she got back to the hotel where she was staying Ben Shaw, her manager, and his publicity agent, Jeff Adams, had arranged a press conference for later that day.

Kip was under no illusions. Ben Shaw was a businessman, pure and simple. After her poor showing in the heats he hadn't even bothered attending the final. But now that she had won he was ready to exploit her fully.

'If the media want to interview you, kid, then you don't say no,' he informed Kip in no uncertain terms.

Kip, who *had* just said no, wasn't so easily cowed. 'I don't like interviews.'

'Who does?' Shaw dismissed her reason as irrelevant.

'Now's the time to cash in,' Jeff Adams put in. 'While you're an overnight sensation. You know what they're calling you? "The Girl from Nowhere". What an angle! We'll have to prepare a biography handout to give them.'

Kip could barely hide her distaste. 'Won't that make me the Girl from Somewhere?' she responded in a sarcastic vein.

Ben Shaw took her literally, saying, 'Don't worry! We can always invent a little mystery if needs be... Just make sure *we* know everything before the press does. I want no skeletons rattling around in the closet, waiting to scare off our deal, or any other sponsors we might attract on the back of this win.'

This time Kip made no reply. Did her father's drinking constitute a skeleton? Or her brief affair with a college professor?

Ben Shaw read her changing expression and said, 'So are there any?'

Kip's face became shuttered. She had no desire to entrust her secrets to these men. She was no longer sure if she and they were even on the same side.

Neither, perhaps, was Ben Shaw, for he felt it necessary to add, 'Remember, kid, you're under contract to me, and short of shooting yourself in the foot you can't get out of it. Maximising your sponsorship potential is part of that deal, so, whether you like it or not, in an hour you will be giving an interview to whoever cares to listen.'

Kip's heart sank. Why had she allowed herself to fall in with Shaw?

It had all happened quite quickly. A year ago she'd returned to Radford, determined that one day she would pay Whit Delaney back. At first she hadn't seen running as the way to do it. Training had been more a distraction from misery than a means to an end. She hadn't expected to be surpassing her best times by the Christmas, a year after her accident.

A few wins at college level and she'd been invited to compete at an indoor event at Easter. She'd come away with a five-figure prize and realised that this was her most likely chance of paying back Whit. She had also attracted the notice of Ben Shaw. She had left Radford shortly afterwards, having mailed most of her prize money on to Maine, and had gone to live at Shaw's training camp.

It was a life not so different from that of a pure-bred racehorse, with a strict diet and exercise programme. Though once she might have settled for it, the regime bored Kip rigid. She did it for the money and the money alone.

So now she couldn't really complain if Ben Shaw saw dollars and cents when he looked at her, and expected her to perform like a circus animal.

She would have to remind herself what the money was for, although that wasn't so easy. Whit Delaney had never cashed that first cheque she'd sent. She'd followed it with a banker's order; he'd torn it up and sent it back to her. Finally she had waited until his father went for a visit to Maine and had given him cash to hand on; that time it had come back as burnt ashes in an envelope. That was when Kip had realised that whatever Whit had felt for her had turned to hate.

If only it could be so simple for her. She tried to hate him, but too many good memories got in the way. She tried to forget him, but Abby kept him alive in her letters. She tried to recover by dating other men, but no one matched up to Whit. She had left Maine loving him and nothing had changed that; as time passed she just grew more used to the pain.

Now she resigned herself to the interview as she changed into a short sleeveless dress provided by Ben Shaw and sat in sufferance as a make-up artist appeared from nowhere to give a hand to nature.

Shaw was pleased with the result, having just noticed her passing resemblance to the young Audrey Hepburn.

Kip just felt unnatural—like a painted doll.

The press conference was to be held in one of their hotel's banquet rooms downstairs. Shaw and Jeff Adams coached her in what answers to give to questions relating to her athletics career, before moving on to her personal life.

'No boyfriend?' Adams checked what he'd already been told.

'No,' Kip replied briefly.

'And your folks are dead, aren't they, kid?' he asked, without even a passing attempt at sensitivity.

Kip nodded.

'So what were they, when they were alive?'

'Is that relevant?'

'Probably not,' Shaw put in, 'if they were nonentities.'

Kip struggled to keep her cool and reminded herself that veryone was a nonentity to Shaw, but pride won out as she eclared, 'They were runners. My mother was a bronze med-list in the World Championships.'

It was a mistake. It made Shaw's day and a cunning smile ppeared on his face. 'Why the hell didn't you tell us this arlier? This could make a great story. Right, Jeff?'

Jeff gave a small nod, before asking her, 'What did your nother die of?'

'Does it matter?'

'You don't want the papers to write the wrong thing, do ou?'

Kip cast a frowning glance between the men. She didn't ike the way things were going. Reluctantly she relayed, Stomach cancer.'

'Yeah, OK.' Shaw seemed to be weighing up its news alue before he asked, 'So who brought you up?'

'My father.'

'And he was a runner too?'

How Kip wished that she'd kept her mouth shut. 'Yes.'

'A medallist?'

'Silver—Commonwealth Games.'

Shaw nodded in satisfaction. 'Well, that certainly gives ou a pedigree, kid. How did *he* die?'

Kip felt herself blushing. 'An illness.'

'What kind of illness?' Shaw sensed that she was hiding omething.

'A liver complaint,' she replied shortly.

It was the truth, but Shaw was nothing if not quick. 'Cir-hosis?'

He stared at Kip but she gave little away. He knew, how-ver.

'Great! Her father was a drunk!' he muttered in disgust to is publicist. 'What are we going to do about that, Jeff?'

Adams gave the question some serious thought. 'We can ry covering up or we can neutralise.'

Meanwhile Kip reeled from the word 'drunk', powerless o retaliate. After all, that was what her father had been.

She eventually found her voice, saying, 'Or we can jus
give the whole thing a miss.'

She got to her feet, intending to walk away from the whol
operation, but Shaw rose too, and barred her path to the doo

'Where do you think you're going?' he demanded. 'Th
interview is in less than ten minutes.'

'And you expect me to reinvent myself in that time?' Sh
raised a challenging brow.

'Don't get cute with me,' Shaw told her.

It was Adams who added, 'I've been thinking, Ben. W
could really turn this to our advantage.'

'What do you mean?' Shaw asked.

'Well, it's almost fashionable these days,' the publici
continued. 'Celebrities having traumatic childhoods, I mean

'I'm not a celebrity!' Kip protested loudly, but was ig
nored.

'It could work for us, yes.' Shaw nodded to himself. 'Let'
see, what angle could we use? She struggled through a child
hood of poverty and abuse, sustained by a dream of runnin
for her country.'

This time Kip was appalled. 'I wasn't abused! You can'
say that!'

'Why not?' Shaw shrugged. 'Your father's in no positio
to deny it, after all.'

Adams smiled at Shaw's attempt at humour. Neither care
about the truth or people's reputations.

Kip had always known that Ben Shaw was no fairy god
mother. She had realised that there would be a price on hi
services; it was only now she discovered that it was just to
high.

She shook her head. 'I won't do this.'

'You have no choice.' Shaw caught her arm before sh
could slip out of the door. 'If you don't believe me, rea
your contract... Jeff!' He nodded to Adams and the othe
man flanked Kip as they went out into the corridor an
walked along to the lift.

Kip fought down a rising panic. She felt as if she wa
being kidnapped, but that was ridiculous. As Shaw said, sh

had signed a contract and was part of this circus. She had to go along with it or...what?

Escape was the obvious answer. It was in her mind when the elevator glided to a halt and they walked out into the hotel lobby. But possibly she would have done nothing about it if fate hadn't taken a strange turn.

At first she didn't believe it. She stopped dead in her tracks and stared in shock. Whit Delaney was sitting in the lobby near the elevators. He stood when he saw her. For a wild moment Kip thought distress had made her hallucinate. He did not really look himself, being dressed immaculately in suit and tie, but there was no mistaking the handsome face and creased blue eyes.

He didn't seem shocked at all, and Kip realised that he had been waiting for her.

Shaw would have steered her away to the banquet room but she dug her heels in.

'Come on, kid, at this stage of the game you can't afford to keep the Press waiting,' he advised her.

But Kip wasn't listening. She'd ceased being aware of him or Adams or anything other than the man walking towards her. How long had it been? A year—a whole year and it was just the same; her heart turned over at the sight of him.

'Kipling.' He said her name and it was like a caress.

She couldn't say anything. She was struggling to contain a range of emotion from fury to delight. Why had he come back? To break her heart all over again?

'I don't know who you are, mister—' Shaw tried to dismiss him '—but Miss Wilson is about to give a press conference.'

Whit seemed oblivious of Shaw. His eyes remained on Kip. 'I was in LA on business. I saw you run on TV.'

And he'd come looking for her, Kip concluded. But why?

'Look, buddy,' Shaw cut in once more, 'Miss Wilson doesn't want to be bothered by fans.'

At this absurdity Kip finally found her voice, saying, 'He isn't a fan.'

'Yes, I am,' he contradicted her. 'I'm one of *Miss Wilson's* biggest fans.'

He slanted her a slow, wry smile that was so familiar that it made twelve months dwindle to the wink of an eye. She was back where she'd been the day she had left his home in Maine. Anyone looking at them could recognise that their relationship had once been intimate.

'Oh, God!' Shaw swore at Kip. 'Don't tell me—this is another skeleton in your goddamn closet. Who else is in there? The whole varsity football team?'

'Watch your mouth, *buddy*.' Whit mocked Shaw's own gangster style of talk, before directing at Kip, 'We have to talk.'

Kip nodded. She knew that it was crazy but she needed to see him again.

He slid a look at Shaw, who was frothing at the mouth. 'Later?'

Kip looked at her manager too, and didn't care. 'No, now.'

'You can't. Not now.' Shaw grabbed her upper arm.

She flinched at his rough handling, and Whit growled at the man, 'Let her go or you'll be testing the quality of the hotel carpet!'

He underlined the threat by taking a step towards Shaw and Kip immediately found herself free.

'Come on.' Whit took her hand and didn't wait around for Shaw to react.

Kip went with him willingly, giggling in surprise, 'You sounded like a gangster.'

'Didn't I just?' he laughed back, then added in an aside, 'Let's just hope I haven't crossed the real thing.'

He hustled her with him, out of the hotel and onto the pavement, and flagged down a passing taxi. They were installed in the back seat before Kip had the chance to wonder where they were going.

'Who was that character?' Whit asked her.

'My manager.' Kip pulled a face, indicating her own dislike of the man. 'Would you really have hit him?'

'I don't know.' Whit shrugged, acknowledging that he wasn't much of a fighter. 'Would you have liked me to?'

'Possibly,' Kip admitted, but her face grew grim as the exhilaration of escape left her.

Whit read her thoughts, saying, 'Have I messed things up for you?'

It would have been easy to blame him, but Kip was nothing if not honest. She'd already been drowning when he'd shown up. He had simply thrown her a lifeline.

'No, I think I was managing that all on my own,' she admitted heavily.

'Want to tell me about it?' His tone put her under no pressure to do so.

Kip shook her head, but barely thirty seconds later spilled the whole story.

'When they found out about my father, they actually thought it would be good publicity. DAUGHTER'S DETERMINATION DESPITE DEAD DIPSO DAD,' she said with black humour.

Whit realised that it was no joke. 'And you find the idea repugnant?'

'Wouldn't anyone?'

'Actually, no; there's many a celebrity who would use it for the sympathy vote.'

'I'm not a celebrity!' she denied adamantly.

'Not at the moment,' he agreed, 'but a few more wins like that and you will be... Did I tell you how brilliant you were, by the way?' he added, a smile in his eyes.

Kip felt her heart fluttering once more, but took refuge in flippancy. 'No, but feel free.'

He laughed, then went on to admit, 'I didn't plan on watching you. Abby told me you'd be racing in LA at the same time as I was here, but I promised myself I wouldn't go to the stadium. Of course, I'd forgotten about cable TV,' he confided with a wry twist to his mouth.

'Do you mind about my letters to Abby?' Kip asked quietly.

He shook his head. 'She wanted to write to you. I'm grate-

ful you wrote back.' He obviously understood her reasons
she had not wanted to hurt the child.

His reasons were less evident. Why had he come to see
her now? It was odd, but she'd always imagined that if they
met again it would be as enemies, or possibly just as strang-
ers. Yet it felt so familiar, sitting here in this taxi with him
Perhaps it was because he knew her in ways that no one else
did.

She looked out of the taxi and finally thought to ask
'Where are we going?'

'Nowhere,' he related. 'I told the driver just to tour round
Where do you want to go?'

Kip didn't know. 'I can't go back to my hotel. Not yet
anyway.'

'Come to mine, then,' he said, and so that there would be
no misunderstanding added, 'We can have dinner together
and plan your next move.'

'I won't do interviews.' Kip practised what she was going
to say to Shaw. 'I just want to run.'

'Then stick to your guns,' Whit told her. 'If it's not in
your contract, you can't be forced to be a publicity machine.'

'I…' Kip fell silent.

He slid her a glance and caught her biting her lip. 'You
did read your contract, didn't you?'

'I can read now, you know!' she responded touchily.

'I wasn't suggesting otherwise,' he countered coolly. 'My
father said you were well on your way to a college degree
when you threw it all up.'

Kip read criticism in his words and flashed him a resentful
look.

He ignored it as he ran on, 'The question wasn't whether
you *could* read your contract—it was whether you *did* read
it. Or, better still, did you get a lawyer to read it?'

'Your father checked it for me,' she announced defensively.

'Oh, that's swell,' he drawled back. 'As a legal eagle, my
father makes a great literature professor.'

Kip glared in anger. 'He was trying to help!'

'I'm sure he was,' Whit agreed on a conciliatory note. 'And there's no point in worrying about that now. I doubt Shaw will force you to abide by any publicity clauses once he realises you'll be a disaster in that direction.'

'Thanks!' Kip snapped, wondering if he had to be so blunt.

'Well, let's face it,' he ran on, 'someone asks your name and you think it's an invasion of your privacy. How are you going to cope with worldwide media attention?'

She wasn't. Kip realised that now. But she was loath to admit it and withdrew instead into brooding silence.

Whit threw her another glance, then, shaking his head, leaned forward to give their cab driver directions.

Kip was left to ponder her next move. Perhaps Whit was right. Shaw couldn't force her. He could just dump her from his team.

Would that be so awful? The question crept into Kip's head and wouldn't creep out again. What would it be like? No more Shaw. No more training. No more running. Just simply step off the treadmill and stand in one place for a while. It suddenly seemed as if she'd spent her whole life on the move. Would it be so awful to stand still?

Deep in thought, Kip remained silent until they arrived at his hotel. It was several income brackets above the one she'd been occupying. As they stepped from their taxi a limousine drew up beside them and out stepped a film star so famous that even Kip recognised her.

Kip managed to stop herself staring like a goggle-eyed schoolgirl, but her mouth did drop open when the star gave a smiling nod in Whit's direction before going inside with her escort.

'Do you know her?' Kip asked him.

'Not well.' He shrugged with little interest. 'She was a friend of my ex-wife's, that's all.'

The woman's fame clearly left him unimpressed. Perhaps that wasn't surprising. He had, after all, been married to a film star.

He took her by the elbow and guided her into the foyer. It was early for dinner but the lobby was already buzzing with theatre-goers dressed in dinner suits and glamorous gowns. Kip was suddenly conscious of her own clothes. Her dress, a simple-cut A-line in a jade colour that matched her eyes, was smart but not evening wear.

She pulled at his sleeve and brought him to a halt before they reached the dining room. 'I can't eat here. I'm not dressed right.'

'You look fine to me.' His eyes never left her face. He clearly didn't give a damn what she was wearing.

Kip glanced through the glass doors to the other diners and knew that she was going to feel out of place. 'I don't want to eat in there.'

'All right.' He bowed to her wishes and suggested, 'We can go to my room and have dinner sent up.'

'What?' Kip's eyes rounded.

He smiled at her look of outrage. 'Well, if you don't feel you can trust me...or yourself,' he added in an undertone loud enough for her to hear.

'You think a lot of yourself, don't you?' she accused him, angry at how little he thought of her.

'No, I've just come to accept this thing between us isn't going to go away,' he answered quietly.

Kip blushed before denying hotly, 'There's nothing between us.'

'OK, prove it,' he countered. 'Come upstairs to my room and have dinner. I won't lay a finger on you, if you don't want me to. We can sit at opposite ends of a table and make polite conversation, and, after the meal's over, say our goodbyes in a civilised manner. And that'll be it—the last time I bother you.'

Last time. The words echoed in Kip's head and gripped tight her heart. It had taken so very long to get over their parting a year ago. Why had he had to look her up and start the pain all over again?

'I...' She knew that she should walk away. She knew that she couldn't risk going upstairs with him for the final chapter.

'I won't touch you,' he repeated quietly, even as he curled strong fingers round her elbow.

She didn't pull away, didn't protest as he led her into the lift, didn't turn tail and run as they walked the length of a corridor.

It wasn't a dream. It was real. Going with him to his room. Rooms. He had a suite. She bypassed a plush sofa and chairs and crossed to the large glass window that overlooked the LA skyline. It was still light but the sun had gone down.

'Do you want dinner now or will you have a drink first?' He opened the mini-bar. 'I have whisky, gin, vodka, Martini…or I can call Room Service?'

Kip turned from the window. She didn't want a drink. She knew that she couldn't eat. She needed it to be over—no more partings, each more painful that the last.

She knew how it must end. She didn't dress it up or give it a more respectable form.

In a quiet but oddly steady voice, she said, 'I'll sleep with you.'

Whit stared back at her, wondering if he'd heard right. 'What?'

'I'll sleep with you,' she repeated, with the same deadly serious expression, and when he failed to respond, she added almost angrily, 'That's what you want, isn't it?'

'I…yes, it is.' Whit was shocked into honesty too. 'Are you always this direct?'

He clearly didn't like it, but Kip didn't care. She didn't want any romance that might lull her into thinking that this was anything more than sex.

'I don't want dinner,' she added, 'and you know I'm no good at small talk.'

'So let's just get on with it?' Whit asked, astounded.

'I want it over,' Kip replied grimly.

Whit finally understood. 'Like a tooth being pulled? You think that'll be it? The pain will go?'

Kip coloured as he made a fairly accurate guess at the way it felt, wanting him, needing him.

'I'll leave if that's what you prefer.' She didn't wait for an answer, passing him on her way to the door.

She opened the door, only to have it slammed shut as he

came up behind her. 'Damn you, you know it isn't,' he grated out, dragging her round to face him. 'I just don't like being thought of as some kind of disease.'

More like a fever, Kip thought as he put his hands to her waist and his closeness sent a shiver down her spine.

'But it's not going to stop me.' His voice softened with his eyes. 'Nothing's going to stop me this time.'

'I…' Kip's throat went suddenly dry. She felt control of the situation slipping away from her.

He bent his head towards her and kissed her on the mouth. Her heart stirred deep within her. He raised his head and their eyes met and caught, and the ground was cut from beneath her.

Her feeling had no name. It was like floating or flying or soaring, free as a bird, yet at the same time being trapped by invisible cords binding her to this man. He took off his jacket and lifted her in his arms. She couldn't break free, didn't want to, as he carried her wordlessly to the other room.

He set her down beside the bed, his eyes still holding hers. Any last bravery deserted Kip. Shyness shaded her cheek-bones and she looked away.

He frowned, registering the change, and in part understood, crossing to draw the curtains and shut out the light.

In darkness it was easier to forget. He came back to her and Kip trembled as he put an arm round her back and un-zipped her dress, then slid it down her slender frame until it dropped to the floor. He did not remove her silk camisole or briefs, but stripped off his own shirt and tie. He threw them on a chair, then bent down and slipped her sandals from her feet. He straightened to kick off his own shoes.

It wasn't cold but Kip shivered all the same as he undid the button and unzipped his trousers, stepping out of them and tossing them in a careless heap on the chair.

Kip was glad of the darkness as they stood there, naked except for their underwear.

He had done everything wordlessly, calmly, without hurry. It suggested a detachment that made Kip want to cry. She asked herself what she'd expected. She was the one whose approach had been clinical, who had not wanted love or romance to confuse this act into anything other than sex. Oh, but her heart ached that it had to be like this!

Then he reached out to her and drew her soft body against his, and everything changed. He wrapped his arms round her and just held her there, suffusing her with his warmth and strength. Fears and doubts slipped away as he buried his face in her hair and whispered hoarsely, 'God, how I want you.'

Another woman would have demanded the word 'love', but not Kip. She didn't want to hear any loving lies. What he felt for her was, in some small part, what she felt for him: a deep, elemental desire that shook her with its intensity.

His lips touched her forehead, her eyes, her cheek, seeking her mouth, finding it in the gentlest of kisses that left her needing more.

'Please.' She breathed the word against his lips.

He breathed something back. It was muffled, but Kip still heard his words. 'I love you.' And her hands went into fists against his chest.

Whit cursed his mistake as she spat back, 'Liar,' and would have twisted from his grip if he hadn't held her tight. He wouldn't let her go—not this time, not now. When she tried to tear her mouth from his he lifted a hand and held the back of her head, forcing her to accept the kiss. She kept struggling but Whit ignored it. He knew that she still wanted him, for even as she struck at him she opened her mouth and moaned aloud as they began to taste each other.

All the time they kissed she hit out at him, straining like a wild thing in his arms. In the back of his mind he knew that if she kept fighting he would have to let her go, but it did nothing to kill his desire for her. He had to have her. She was right. It was an ache that had to be cured—or at least deadened.

He kissed her and she kissed him back, but still she fought him with her arms and her fists until finally Whit forced himself to stop. He dragged his mouth from hers and struggled for control. His breathing was ragged. So was hers. It filled the silence, the darkness.

'Don't use that word!' she told him hoarsely.

He came back with, 'Is it so terrifying—to be loved?'

'What's love?' Kip couldn't believe he felt such for her.

But her heart hammered all the harder as a hand reached up to touch her face. 'Let me show you.'

A low, persuasive murmur, his voice curled round Kip's senses, cheating her of her anger. She still didn't believe, but, oh, God, she wanted to. When he lifted his other arm to cradle her face, she felt too weak to pull away.

'Yes?' He made it her decision.

And all pride deserted her.

She echoed, 'Yes,' in a small, unsteady voice, and 'Yes,' again as his mouth came down on hers and breathed life into her once more.

Kip no longer tried to hold onto her head—or her heart. He kissed her hard and she kissed him back, her arms sliding over his bare chest.

Whit felt her body soft and trembling against his, and, putting his hands to her waist, dragged her even closer. He kissed her harder until she opened her lips wider and let him invade more deeply the sweet, secret places of her mouth. He meant to go slow. He didn't want her to be cured. He wanted to feed the ache, to make her want him the way he wanted her.

They fell onto the bed together, mouths still locked, limbs entwined. She felt so slight and breakable in his arms, but her passion was strong and consuming and her body was fire. His control was virtually gone. He wanted her so badly that he could have entered her then. He had to roll away from her, put some space between her damp, soft skin and his.

Kip was bereft. She lay on her back, her body suddenly cold to the bone. Was he rejecting her? Paying her back for running away from him last year? Silent seconds passed, and she wanted to curl up and die.

Then a hand reached across to take hers and pull her round to face him. Her eyes, adjusted to the darkness, met and caught his. This was no rejection, she realised as he traced her features with long, gentle fingers.

'You're beautiful,' he said, almost as if it came as a surprise to him.

Kip shook her head. How could he find her beautiful when he'd been married to one of the most beautiful women in the world?

Yet his eyes told her that he did and he watched her face all the time he touched her, stroking her soft body, smoothing a hand over the silk of her camisole, slowly unlacing the ties, brushing against the silk of her skin.

He watched her as he pushed aside the garment to cup her small breast in his large hand, and, with his thumb, made the nipple stand out from the dark areola. She shut her eyes, but knew that he still watched her as he brushed her other breast with the back of his hand, gently arousing the other nipple.

She kept her eyes shut as he pushed her back against the counterpane of the bed. She waited for him to touch her again. This time it was his mouth, and she betrayed herself completely, moaning aloud as his tongue made slow, sensuous circles round the swollen peak of her breast. Over and over he licked and played, gently at first, then more roughly, as she responded with small pleasure noises and the shift of her body beneath his.

Desire became pain, writhing like a snake through her belly. Then his hand moved in a slow trail downwards, making her wait, making her want, as it slid over the silk of her briefs and back, over and back, until it slid between, seeking, finding, warm and moist, ready for the slip of his long fingers, gentle, knowing, pleasuring, unbelievable...

He kissed her as she gasped for him. He kept touching her as she gasped. He kept touching her until her breath was coming hard and fast, and he felt that he could wait no longer.

Kip opened her eyes when he stopped kissing her, and saw him, poised above her, his face etched with desire for her.

She cried out as finally he entered her, but it wasn't with pain so much as shock. He filled her so completely. She lay still for a moment, feeling as if he might tear her apart. Then he began to move inside her, slowly at first, and her eyes opened wide at the stark pleasure of it.

Whit sensed rather than saw the wonder on her face, and knew the truth. There had been no others, just him. It didn't stop him—he couldn't have stopped if he'd tried.

And Kip—for her, making love to this man was as natural as breathing. It required no thought, yet she was aware of everything—the warmth of his body, the sweat on his skin, the very male scent of him, the strong, hard thrust of his manhood, giving pleasure she could never have imagined.

It was as natural as running, only different, because she wasn't on her own. He was running with her. He was making her part of him, and himself part of her. They breathed together, held each other, crossed the line at the exact same moment. And this time she knew that she'd won as he called out her name, hoarse but clear, half-curse, half-cry.

The feeling of being one didn't go away. She didn't let it. She shook her head when he would have talked. She lay in his arms and listened to the beat of his heart and refused to allow reality any place in this darkened room.

He took his lead from her. They did not talk of feelings or future or the year they had lost. Instead they made love, and slept, and made love again, as if each hoped that they could cure the ache that way.

CHAPTER ELEVEN

KIP woke in the morning with the first sign of light filtering through the hotel curtains. She could easily have shut her eyes again, but day brought with it reality.

She gazed at the man lying in the bed beside her, and knew then that she'd been kidding herself. If anything, last night had made things ten times worse.

She had to face the truth. She'd been in love with Whit Delaney when she'd run from him last summer. She was in love with him now. She was always going to be in love with him.

But nothing else had changed either. She could go back to Maine and live with him—a week, a month, a year—knowing that one day it must end. Or she could go now, retrieve her pride and spare herself the watching and waiting and grieving for the first sign that he was tiring of her.

She tried to slip from his arms but his hold on her tightened. He was still half-asleep. She murmured about needing to go to the bathroom and managed to gain her freedom that way. She dressed quietly in the other room, but couldn't resist going back through for one last look.

She left him a note. She kept it brief and factual. Then she slipped away, her heart breaking.

It took all her nerve to walk through the lobby of his hotel. At just past six in the morning only the staff were around. She looked straight ahead as she sailed through Reception, clearly wearing yesterday's clothes.

She walked through the streets, feeling like some lady of the night, and did another stare-straight-ahead job when she reached her own hotel. She managed to avoid any eye contact but felt tainted by the time she reached her room. She showered and put on a dressing gown.

In a couple of hours she would dress and pack. For now she curled up on an armchair and thought of last night. She felt no shame. She had hurt no one but herself, and she'd always known how it would be.

Love was no hearts and flowers and happy-ever-afters for her. It was a stolen moment that brought pain and tears and a longing that wasn't going to go away. How naïve to think that sleeping with him would offer a cure. Instead it had made her condition terminal. She had gained too many memories, and now, what other than pride would keep her from Whit's bed any time he chose?

Distance was the only answer, and with that in mind she dressed and started to pack. She was almost finished when there was a knock on the door. She opened it to Ben Shaw.

'Where have you been?' He pushed past her into the room. 'I've been looking for you since last night.'

Kip flushed. She didn't want Ben Shaw to know she'd slept elsewhere.

'Old boyfriend, was he?'

'Pardon?'

'The guy in the lobby yesterday,' Ben Shaw sneered. 'If I'd known you like the mature type, I might have tried my own luck.'

Kip didn't hide her distaste. 'Have you something important to say? If not, I have to finish my packing.'

Shaw's face tightened. 'So high and mighty, but I could drop you just like that.' He snapped his fingers and smiled once more as he enjoyed his power over her.

But he had none, he discovered, as Kip responded, 'Feel free. I don't want to run any more.'

'What?' He looked at her in disbelief.

'I'm tired of running,' she claimed quite seriously. 'There's more to life than going in endless circles.'

'Is this some kind of joke?' Shaw's eyes questioned her sanity. 'You can't be tired of running. We're about to make the big time.'

Kip shook her head. "Fraid not. You'll have to find another racehorse to back,' she told him flippantly, and, crossing back to her case, snapped the locks. She picked it and her handbag up off the bed.

Shaw finally realised that she wasn't playing a game. He followed her to the door and, coming up behind her, slammed it shut before she could properly open it.

'You can't walk out on me. No one walks out on me,' he shouted furiously.

Kip took a step away from him and the door, and wondered how best to calm him down.

'Someone's made you a better offer,' he accused her, making a grab for her arm. 'That's it, isn't it?'

'No, it's nothing like that,' Kip denied, trying and failing to twist from his hold.

She knew a moment's fear as he tightened his grip and made her wince. His face contorted in an expression of viciousness. He was deliberately causing her pain.

Kip was wondering how best to extricate herself from the situation when there was a knock at the door, in answer to her silent prayer.

'Kip, is the boss in there?' It was the voice of her trainer, Steve Clark.

'Steve,' she shouted back in relief, 'hold on. I'll open the door.'

For a moment Ben Shaw looked as if he was going to stop her. He was clearly enjoying his control and her fear. But then he suddenly released her and pushed her from him.

Kip didn't hang around. She opened the door as quickly as she was able. 'Come in, Steve,' she invited with some urgency.

'Boss.' Steve Clark acknowledged the other man with a nod before glancing back at her flushed face. 'Are you OK, Kip?'

'No, she's not!' Shaw answered for her. 'She's goddamn crazy. She's quitting.'

'Quitting?' her trainer echoed. 'Quitting what?'

'Running—what else?' Shaw growled at him, then moderated his tone slightly as he added, 'Speak to her, Steve. She's got five minutes to change her mind, or we're out of here and she's history.'

Shaw walked out, slamming the door behind him.

Steve Clark turned to her in disbelief. 'Tell me it isn't true.'

Kip felt guilty but resolute. 'I'm sorry, Steve.'

'But why?'

'I just don't want to run any more.'

'Is it Shaw?' Steve Clark guessed. 'I know you've been giving him the run-around and that's fine by me, but you can't just walk out on him. If you do, he can make sure you'll never race again.'

'I don't care.' Kip went to pick up the case she'd dropped on the floor. 'I know I'm letting you down and I am sorry, Steve, but racing no longer seems important.'

Steve Clark heard the lack of interest in her voice and knew that it was hopeless. Without commitment and a passion to win, she would be just another also-ran.

He let her go, and Kip escaped before Shaw could return. She went down in the lift and made for the street door. She was almost there when a hand caught her and pulled her up. She wheeled round, expecting to see Shaw. Instead her heart lifted at the sight of Whit.

It sank fairly rapidly as he growled, 'That damn fool of a deskman wouldn't call you. I've been kicking my heels down here for two hours... What the hell did you think you were doing, walking out like that?'

He was almost shouting. It drew several stares and the appearance of the assistant manager.

'Can I help you, madam?' he directed at Kip.

Kip frowned. How could he help her? No one could.

'Miss?' the assistant continued, waiting for her instruction.

'Miss doesn't need your help,' Whit barked at him. 'Miss is more than capable of wiping the floor with you, me or anyone else that stands in her way. Right?'

'Oh, yeah, right!' Kip's temper rose to meet the occasion. 'And you're just a victim, I suppose!'

The assistant manager looked from one angry face to the other, decided that they deserved one another and hastily withdrew.

Whit grabbed her arm and her bag and hustled Kip towards the relative privacy of the hotel lounge.

'Let me go!' Kip winced at the hard fingers digging into her elbow.

'Forget it!' he grated back. 'You've run out on me one time too many… I should have known. Hidden your clothes or something. Tied you to the bedpost.'

Kip coloured as he alluded to the night they'd spent together, but she said nothing in reply. He pushed her down on an armchair in a corner and sat in a chair opposite.

Whit took a deep, steadying breath before continuing, 'Do you know how it felt—waking up to find you gone?'

No worse, Kip imagined, than the going itself. 'I left you a note.'

'Oh, yeah, it was some note!' He took the offending article from his jacket and read aloud, '"Had to go. Plane to catch. Will send on money." For a second I thought you were planning on paying for my *services*,' he added with a harsh, humourless laugh.

Kip went even redder. 'I meant the hospital fees you paid. I can pay you some out of my prize money.'

'Don't worry, I understood,' he went on, eyes stormy. 'You think paying me back is going to make me disappear.'

Kip wished that it could be that simple. He was in her head now and he always would be. Why did he have to come after her and make things that much more difficult?

'I have to go for my plane.' She repeated what had been in the note.

'Just like that? You've taken the *cure*—' his lips twisted on the word '—and now it's back on track.'

Why was he doing this? Why put them through it?

'What do you want, Whit?' she asked in a weary voice.

'Right at the moment,' he grated back, 'I think I want to hit you.'

His eyes told her that he meant it. Kip felt his anger coming in waves. She hadn't expected this reaction. She discounted it as pride.

'And after that?' Kip challenged him to admit that they had nothing real to offer each other.

'And after that,' he echoed, holding her eyes, 'I want to take you upstairs to bed and make love to you. I want to listen to you moan when I touch you. I want to hear you cry my name when I—'

'Stop it!' Kip jumped to her feet, unwilling to listen to more.

'Why?' He stood with her and grabbed her arm. 'Don't you like being reminded that you're human? That you can feel like anyone else? That you might even love? Or was last night all pretence?'

The word 'yes' formed on her lips but she just couldn't say it. It seemed as if he knew the truth anyway. Why else would he talk of love?

'Let me go, Whit.' Her tone was defeated. She couldn't take much more of this emotional battering.

'I can't,' he told her simply. 'Don't you see? I can't.'

Kip raised her eyes to his, questioning what he meant. Whit stared back at her, not hiding anything.

For a single moment the truth lay between them. They reached out for it, but it slipped through their fingers as another voice entered the conversation.

It was Steve Clark again. 'The deskman said you were still here. Have you changed your mind?'

Kip shook her head. 'I'm sorry, Steve.'

The trainer looked from Kip to Whit and back again, and said in resignation, 'OK. Look after yourself, kid, and if you ever want an "in" again give us a call and I'll try to talk Shaw around.'

'Thanks, Steve,' Kip called after him as he rushed off to catch the plane.

'What was all that about?' Whit asked, frowning.

'I've quit,' Kip admitted with some reluctance.

'You've quit?' He looked at her in disbelief. 'You mean you've quit Shaw's operation?'

Kip nodded, then thought to add, 'I'll be able to pay you back something from my win yesterday, but I'm afraid you'll have to wait a while for the rest.'

'To hell with that!' Whit dismissed impatiently. 'I don't care about the money.'

'No—' Kip realised that '—but I do.'

He shook his head at her stubbornness. 'You know what I did with the last money you sent me?'

'You burnt it,' she recalled bitterly.

'Uh-uh.' He shook his head. 'I donated it to an adult-literacy centre. I assumed you'd appreciate the cause.'

'But—' Kip frowned '—your father gave me an envelope of ashes.'

'Just paper,' he confessed with a grimace. 'What you might call a dramatic gesture. I wanted you to get the message and not send any more.'

Kip supposed that it was better that he hadn't burnt it. At least her money had gone to a worthwhile cause.

'Why have you given up running—' he returned to the real issue '—when everything's going your way?'

'Not my way,' she said, shaking her head. 'I didn't have a way. It was my father's—his plan, his dream. I never had one of my own. You said as much.'

'Perhaps.' He had always recognised that her running was more an obsession than a passion. 'And have you now?'

Kip could so easily have said that *he* was the new dream—having him, holding him, loving him for a lifetime—but it seemed nearer fantasy.

'I thought I might go back to college,' she said, surprising herself.

'Radford,' he concluded.

She shook her head. There were too many memories at Radford.

'There are some fine colleges in Maine,' he added. 'Perhaps I could help you find a place this fall.'

Kip gave him a pained look. Did he think that she'd want to be so close to him? It would only make things worse.

'I can manage by myself,' she said defensively.

'Lucky you,' he replied in an undertone.

It drew Kip's eyes to his face. He looked tired rather than angry.

She felt the need to say, 'I *am* grateful.'

His lips quirked. 'God, that's a real killer. Gratitude.'

'I don't know what else you want of me,' she threw back

'Don't you?' He lifted a mocking brow. 'Well, I would show you, only it's kinda public around here.'

His look told her what he wanted. Her. She'd been right in one way. Last night had not diminished his desire.

Colouring, she snapped, 'Is that all you can think of?'

'Currently,' he said without excuse. 'The disease turned out to be fatal—no cure.'

What was he saying? Kip didn't dare hope.

'Still, in forty years, who knows?' he ran on. 'I might just settle for pipe and slippers and linament rubbed in my joints... Care to find out?'

'I—I...' Kip was losing this conversation somewhere. 'Are you...?'

'Proposing? Yes.'

'Marriage?'

'That was the general idea.'

Kip continued to gape at him. He was joking. He had to be. It certainly sounded as if his tongue was very firmly in his cheek.

'Give it time. It might grow on you,' he continued in the same vein.

Kip didn't want time to consider it. She abruptly stood and would have walked away if he hadn't caught her arm.

'Let me go!' Red pinpoints of anger highlighted her cheeks.

His own temper was on the rise too. 'Should I take it the answer is no?'

'What do you think?' she snapped in reply.

'May I ask why?' he demanded.

'Because it's absurd,' she exploded back at him. 'You don't marry people just because you want to keep having sex with them.'

'I can think of worse reasons,' he responded drily, and found himself talking to thin air.

Kip had wrested her arm from his, and, abandoning her case, headed for escape. He caught her in the lobby. Before she could struggle, he pulled her towards a telephone booth and forced her inside. He followed after her, giving her no room to move at all.

'The desk staff are looking at us.' She saw them through the glass.

'So?' He obviously didn't give a damn.

'Let me out!' she spat at him.

'Shut up,' he growled back, 'and listen. You're right; if it were only sex, then marriage would be a crazy idea. But are you so certain it is? Have you ever really given love a chance?'

'What?' Kip stared at him, open-mouthed.

'Yeah, I know, I sound like some character in a romantic novel.' His mouth twisted in self-derision. 'Put it down to desperation. Any second you're going to walk out of my life once more and I can't think what to do about it.'

Kip continued to stare up at him, wondering if one of them was going mad. 'What are you saying?'

'I reckon that's pretty obvious.' He looked more angry than anything as he declared, 'I love you. I don't want to lose you.'

'I…you…' Kip just didn't believe it. 'You can't…'

'That's what I told myself,' he replied with a grimace. 'You can't love someone who treats you like something she found under a stone, but it's made little difference. I guess love defies reason.'

It certainly did. That this man could love her… Kip shook her head. She could hardly take it in.

He touched her gently on the cheek, and it triggered off all the emotion she'd been containing for so long.

'You're crying… God, Kipling, don't cry.' A long finger came out and caught the tear slipping down her cheek.

'I can't help it. It's been so horrible,' Kip confessed at his deepening frown. 'Loving you, I mean, and thinking you could never feel the same, but still wanting to…well, you know what. And I hadn't. Not with anyone else. I don't suppose you'll believe me, but—'

'I was the first—I realised that. You love me?' he queried, wanting to hear the words that really mattered.

'I—I…yes,' she admitted, as if it were the guiltiest of secrets.

His smile flashed on briefly, then switched to perplexity. 'But if that's true then why…?' He trailed off as he tried to make sense of her past behaviour.

'I didn't want to love you,' she declared in protest. 'I mean, it wasn't likely you'd love me back, was it?'

Whit looked at her as if she were mad, as if loving her was as inevitable as night following day. Then he kissed her, soft and slow, on the mouth, conveying his feelings more effectively than words.

Kip's heart leapt as it always did, only this time there was joy rather than fear in responding. She kissed him back until love and desire were inseparable.

'Let's go back to my hotel.' His intention was clear.

Kip nodded. She wasn't going to pretend. She needed him too.

She forgot her case and everything else as they made for the exit. They passed the assistant manager, who was clearly hiding a smile. Not half an hour ago they'd been having a stand-up fight in his reception area.

When they were installed in a taxi, Whit said, 'Does this mean the answer's yes?'

'Yes?' Kip didn't remember the question.

'To my proposal,' he reminded her.

Kip wanted to say yes. Shout it, in fact. But there was someone else to consider.

Her silence spoke volumes. Whit felt his stomach hit the floor of the cab. He couldn't lose her now. 'You need time to think about it.'

Kip shook her head. 'It isn't that… It's just—'

'Your running,' he guessed. 'That isn't a problem. If you need to go on—try for that gold—I'll back you all the way.'

'It isn't that.' Kip's worries lay elsewhere. 'It's Abby. It has to be right for her. If it isn't, I can't marry you.'

She was plainly sincere, and Whit recognised it for the selflessness it was. Having suffered an uncertain childhood herself, she would not inflict such on another little girl.

'Trust me; it'll be right.' Whit's conviction was absolute.

His precocious daughter had been well ahead of the game. She had seen the strength and goodness in Kip long before he had.

But Kip herself was a natural pessimist. 'If it isn't, we could…well, we could still be lovers.' She coloured at her own words.

He saw it and smiled. 'We'll always be lovers,' he said, with such certainty that Kip could almost believe it.

Always lovers. It was the same vow that Whit made to her in a Maine church that fall, when his father gave her away and his daughter was a proud, smiling bridesmaid. The same vow he made after the first year, though Kip knew that she wasn't always the easiest person to live with. The same vow he would make every year as their love grew and flourished and Kip realised that she didn't have to run away from life, or love, any more.

Harlequin Romance®

Delightful
Affectionate
Romantic
Emotional

Tender
Original

Daring
Riveting
Enchanting
Adventurous
Moving

Harlequin Romance® —
capturing the world you dream of...

HARLEQUIN®
Makes any time special ®

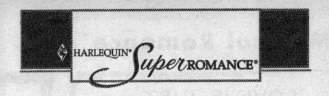
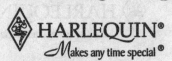

Medical Romance™

LOVE IS JUST A HEARTBEAT AWAY!

New in North America, **MEDICAL ROMANCE** brings you four passionate stories every month... each set in the action and excitement of big-city hospitals and small-town medical practices. Devoted doctors, sophisticated surgeons, compassionate nurses—you'll meet this group of dedicated medical professionals in this thrilling series. Their fast-paced world and intense emotions are guaranteed to provide you with hours and hours of reading pleasure.

To find out more about this exciting new series, contact our toll free customer service number: 1-800-873-8635 and reference #4542 when calling. You won't find it in bookstores!

HARLEQUIN®
Makes any time special ®

Visit us at www.eHarlequin.com

MEDDIRA

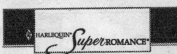

HARLEQUIN®
Makes any time special ®

Upbeat,
All-American Romances

Duets™

Romantic Comedy

**Harlequin®
Historical**

Historical,
Romantic Adventure

HARLEQUIN®
INTRIGUE

Romantic Suspense

Harlequin Romance ®

Capturing the World
You Dream Of

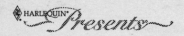

Seduction and passion
guaranteed

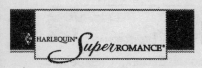

Emotional,
Exciting, Unexpected

Sassy, Sexy, Seductive!

HARLEQUIN®
INTRIGUE

WE'LL LEAVE YOU BREATHLESS!

If you've been looking for thrilling tales of contemporary passion and sensuous love stories with taut, edge-of-the-seat suspense—then you'll love Harlequin Intrigue!

Every month, you'll meet four new heroes who are guaranteed to make your spine tingle and your pulse pound. With them you'll enter into the exciting world of Harlequin Intrigue— where your life is on the line and so is your heart!

THAT'S INTRIGUE— ## ROMANTIC SUSPENSE ## AT ITS BEST!

HARLEQUIN®
Makes any time special ®

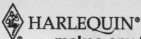